D1606071

# ASHES

## Kenzo Kitakata

Translated by Emi Shimokawa

VERTICAL.

Published by Vertical, Inc., New York.

Originally published in Japanese as *Bo no kanashimi* by Shinchosha, Tokyo, 1990.

ISBN 1-932234-02-0

Manufactured in the United States of America

*Book design by Studio 5E*

First American Edition

Vertical, Inc.
257 Park Avenue South, 8th Floor
New York, NY 10010
www.vertical-inc.com

# CONTENTS

Part One

# THE MAN WITHIN

# W I N D

Inside, it was dark. A few scattered pools of light highlighted the darkness. The man walked straight across the room and headed for the bar.

"Lose the jazz," he said, in a low but penetrating voice.

Apart from his voice, he seemed ordinary enough: gray suit, understated tie, close-cropped hair. To look at him, anyone would have assumed he was just another company man who'd dropped in for a quick drink.

"I can't stand jazz. Didn't you know that?"

The bartender smiled, but said nothing. The man rested an elbow on the counter and turned toward the billiard table, a faint smile on his lips.

A shaded canopy light hung over the table, shining down on the green baize and the balls that rolled across it.

The only other illuminated area was a 2-foot circle of light cast onto the counter from a spotlight in the ceiling. It was where the bartender mixed his drinks so that rainbow-colored concoctions would look dazzling.

It gave away that the place was new.

The bar counter and the stools in front of it were made of old recycled wood. Someone had gone to the effort of staining all the light bulbs brown with what may or may not have been real cigarette tar.

The sharp crack of billiard balls echoed across the room, and music came on again as if to drown out the sound.

"This all you got?" the man said. The air of ordinariness that hung around him vanished the second he opened his mouth to speak.

"But this isn't jazz, sir."

"No, it's even noisier."

"You'd prefer something a little quieter, I take it?"

"Something like that."

"I'll put something slow on next, then, soon as this track gets done."

The man nodded, and deep lines appeared in the skin around his neck. The wrinkles in his face, too, were more pronounced when he spoke.

"Bourbon soda," he said, still looking over at the billiard table. The bartender fell silent, and placed a glass on the counter.

From the billiard table there came the sound of balls sliding into pockets, followed by a smattering of applause. The man turned back to the counter and reached for his glass.

"What bourbon do you use?"

"Four Roses. Usually do, 'less the customer asks specifically for something else."

"Not bad."

Another ripple of applause drifted over from the billiard table, but this time the man didn't bother to look.

The bartender placed a cocktail glass on the counter, where it glinted in the spotlight that shone from the ceiling. He whipped down bottles, barely checking the label, and poured from each into a cocktail shaker. It was only when he poured that he seemed to take care.

He got to work mixing the drinks, and for a while the rattling of the shaker drowned out the sound of clacking billiard balls.

A pale blue liquid streamed down into the shimmering glass on the counter.

"So that's all there is to it, huh?"

"To what, sir?"

"Cocktails."

"I do something wrong?"

"Nah. Just too damn fancy for me."

"Well, every place's got its selling point, right?"

"Should be about the taste."

"Well, we are known for that, too."

A waiter came over and put the cocktail on his tray, then carried it away.

"Hey, I thought I told you I don't like jazz."

The bartender looked up as if he'd just remembered, and changed the music.

"What's this?"

"It's from a movie. Pretty old one."

The man nodded, but didn't prompt the bartender for

further details.

"Can't stand jazz."

"I'll try to keep that in mind from now on."

"What, you think I've never been here before?"

"Isn't that the case?"

"I pass this way all the time."

"It's the first time you've actually been inside, though, right?"

"I don't know. Could be."

"We only opened about two months back."

"What're you talking about? This place's been here for at least five years."

"I'm afraid not, sir."

"I'm sure it was here five years ago."

The bartender started to say something, but stopped himself short. The man leaned across the counter.

"Listen. It's been here five years, I'm telling you."

The bartender nodded slightly.

Laughter from the pool table.

The door opened and a woman came in by herself. She stood in the doorway for a while taking the place in and then walked over to the bar.

"Bloody Mary," she said, in a slightly high-pitched voice. Her long fingernails were painted silver. She tapped them lightly against the surface of the counter, as though she were scratching at something.

"Bloody Mary, right?" the bartender said. He sounded much more relaxed and cheerful now than when he was talking to the man.

"Not a bad place you got here," she said.

"Thanks."

"Never even knew of it."

"We just opened a couple months back," the bartender replied, glancing over at the man as he spoke.

"So billiards is the big thing these days, huh?"

"Yeah, actually we wanted to have two tables, but—"

"Takes up more space than you thought? The extra room to cue up and stuff."

"You play yourself?"

"Not really. I only know eight-ball."

"Plenty of people here'll give you a game if you feel like it."

The man pushed his empty glass over to the bartender. Silently, the bartender added ice and poured in some more bourbon, and soda.

"Do it over," the man said, peering into his glass. The woman glanced over at him as if she'd just noticed him.

"I'm sorry?"

"I don't like the way you made it."

"What didn't you like about it?"

"My glass wasn't empty. And it wasn't soda. Melted ice-water."

"So?"

"I asked for a bourbon soda."

"Ice melts, sir."

"I don't need you to tell me that."

The woman looked at the man again. She didn't seem irritated. Simply curious. She lifted a hand to her head and smoothed back her hair with her long, painted fingernails.

"I said do it over."

"But, sir."

"Don't argue with me, kid. Just do it."

"Yes, sir."

The bartender rinsed out the glass. The low, clunking rattle of ice cubes mingled with the clacking of billiard balls.

"The customer's always right," the man said.

"I know. Another bourbon soda, was it?"

"I don't think I like your tone."

"Sorry?"

"Talking to me like you're talking to some kid."

"Surely you're joking, sir."

"I ain't some kid."

"I'm quite aware of that, sir."

"You are, huh? You know, I don't think you are."

"What can I say? You're not drunk, are you?"

"No, I'm not."

The bartender handed him a fresh bourbon soda. The man reached out for it silently.

"How do you like it?"

"I had to tell you how to make it, and you ask me?"

The man squinted as he brought the glass to his lips, as though smoke were stinging his eyes. Tiny fizzing bubbles were bursting from the unstirred bourbon soda.

"How come you didn't stir it?"

"Most people prefer it that way, sir. The soda loses its fizz if you stir it up."

"Looked to me like you didn't think it worth your trouble."

"But that's how I made the first one too, sir."

"That so?"

"You don't like it?"

"I bet you're gonna tell me that's the way you do it here whether I like it or not."

"In a word, sir, yes."

The bartender laughed, and the man smiled faintly too. He looked close to forty when he smiled. Strangely, as the smile faded, he looked younger again.

The woman was staring at him quite openly now, as she sipped at her Bloody Mary.

"Something bothering you?" the man asked.

"Not really. Just had a feeling I'd seen you before."

"Well I don't know you, sister."

"Oh?"

The woman wasn't exactly young. Dressed in black. There was a small silver design the same color as her fingernails sewn across her breast.

"Notice what's playing?" the man asked the bartender.

The film song had finished and the music had changed. The bartender made no move to do anything about it.

"Didn't I tell you twice already I can't stand jazz?"

"The other customers prefer this kind of music. We

can't have a movie soundtrack playing the whole time."

"Well, I don't like jazz. I told you that already. I didn't notice anyone coming over to complain about the movie soundtrack."

"Maybe they were just being polite."

"Nobody's listening anyway. They're all too busy with their game."

"I'm sorry, sir, but you can't have it all your way."

"I don't think I'm asking for much."

"Establishments have to have a certain ambience, and we try to maintain ours."

"You saying I don't fit in with your 'ambience'?"

"To be honest, sir, I think you'd be better off in one of the bars by the station. They'll play movie soundtracks and traditional songs for you all night long if you want them to."

"Okay. I get the message."

"And don't worry about the check, sir. It's on the house."

"You telling me to scram?"

"You can't be comfortable here—with such noisy music playing."

"Step out."

"Huh?"

"That revelry over at the pool table is better for your 'ambience' than me?"

"Well, yes, sir. To put it bluntly."

"Patience, kid. What did you do before you started

here?"

"What's that got to do with you?"

"I said step out. Telling me to scram because I have bad taste, you prick."

"Give me a break, sir."

"Don't make me mad. Please don't make me mad."

"You seem pretty mad already."

"Yeah."

"Don't worry about the check, sir."

The man rose.

"Thinks I do this for free drinks," he muttered. Turning toward the woman, he smiled faintly. Then he turned around and walked over to the billiard table.

A young man stood poised to shoot. Just a kid, probably still in his teens. He looked up and scowled at the man as he came close.

Walking up to the kid, the man held out his hand and grabbed hold of the cue.

"What do you want?" the kid complained, but let go of the stick.

Suddenly the man leapt up onto the billiard table. He swung the cue hard at the lighting over the table. A feast of sound, and the light died. Pool balls shot toward the bar and smashed into bottles lined up behind the bartender. The green baize was trampled. Shouts. The men lounging in the back got on their feet, in unison. They stood up but didn't move toward the man.

The kid whose cue the man had taken was still rooted

to the spot by the table. A shoe sliced the air. The kid went down like timber and sprayed vomit about him.

An instant later, the man had jumped off the table, and the spotlight above the counter was in smithereens. There was no sign of the woman at the bar.

The man held out the cue toward the shelves. Bottles fell, one by one. The bartender let out a few squeals.

The man grinned. He was taking his time. He turned to smashing the wooden stools against the counter.

A waiter hurled himself at the man's waist. In one fluid motion the waiter's body floated and came down on the floor. Openmouthed, he stared up at the man and stayed down on his hands and knees.

The man did no more violence. He walked past the counter slowly and returned the cue to its place in the rack.

He pinched a crest of the trampled green baize lightly with his fingertips. He smiled, but the smile was not there for long.

Jazz was playing in the background. There was no other sound.

"What do I owe you?" the man said, breaking the silence at last. His voice was as low as ever, and he wasn't out of breath. The bartender stood with his mouth open, unanswering.

"Where's my check?"

"Don't worry about it." There was a slight tremble in the bartender's voice.

"I want my check."

The door opened. Another one of the waiters came rushing in with a cop.

"All right Tanaka, take it easy," the cop said. The man he had called Tanaka stood unmoving.

Another cop hurried in through the door. The man nodded and held out his wrists, but instead of cuffing him, they just grabbed him by the arm on each side.

The kid he'd kicked and the waiter he'd flung to the floor were taken along with him.

"Holy shit," the bartender muttered. "What a fucking drunk."

"That man wasn't drunk." It was the woman. She stood by the counter, one hand on it. "You know that, don't you?"

"Two bourbon sodas. Maybe he was just pissed off and looking for trouble."

"He came to destroy this place."

"You think so?"

"When he got up, he had a look on his face—like he had a job to do. Like he didn't really want to do it."

"You mean—"

"Did you piss them off somehow?"

"They demanded a cut of the profits. But I thought that kind of thing was history."

"You'd have gotten off lighter." The woman put a cigarette between her lips—Marlboro Menthols, not a brand you saw every day in Japan. The other customers were starting to talk again, excitedly.

"Not much you can do about it now."

"Come to think of it, the damage isn't that serious. I guess we need to get the table fixed before anyone comes here again to play pool, though."

"I see."

Behind them, the waiter was starting to clean things up. A gust of wind had swept through the place—that's how it seemed.

The music had stopped. The bartender stood shaking his head.

"I'm not gonna take this lying down."

"Well, don't try too hard," the woman advised. Her hands were wrapped around her Bloody Mary, the same one as before.

"Quite an experience—in just our second month," the bartender said.

"I'd be careful."

"You think that wasn't his last visit?"

"Who knows."

"The police will protect us. We pay our taxes."

The woman sat down on a stool. The bartender set down an ashtray in front of her and humphed.

"Fifteen or sixteen bottles broken, not that many," he said. The smell of alcohol was everywhere.

"Wait a minute." The bartender cocked his head. "Uh-oh."

"What?"

"They took that customer. And one of the waiters."

"Why not? Victims of the crime."

"They're high school students."

"High school?"

"Seventeen and eighteen. They're underage. The waiter's only seventeen."

"Oops."

"Maybe the police will want to talk to us."

"Probably close you down for a few months."

"Damn it."

"Maybe that's what he had in mind, that man."

"Shit."

With a shrug, the woman downed what was left of her Bloody Mary. The bartender wasn't looking at the woman anymore. He didn't seem to be looking at anything.

"Maybe he wanted to ruin you."

"Ruin?"

"If that was a 'job' he was doing."

"No."

"Well, the cops knew him. Tanaka, they called him."

"The cops...."

The woman set her empty glass on the counter. Quietly, she ordered another.

The bartender was still staring at nothing.

# PIGEONS

It was a clear day.

The man strolled slowly through the sunshine until he came to a stone bench and eased himself down onto it like an old man. He wasn't young, but he wasn't exactly old either.

Gray suit. After loosening his understated tie a little he sat still, hardly moving.

The lawn sloped away ahead of him. It wasn't empty. Probably a good number of people if one took the trouble to count: sitting on the grass, lying down, enjoying the sunshine. The bench the man was sitting on was at the top of the slope, and all he could see of the people ahead of him were rows of backs. Behind his bench there was nothing but a gravel path and a large building no one ever seemed to go into or come out of.

The man was gazing at a faraway clump of trees—a grove, in fact, judging from the depth of green. People there looked tiny from where he was sitting.

Ten minutes went by when the man, who had been dead still, started. He began to rummage around in his pockets and took out a crumpled pack of Camels; he put one to his mouth. He scratched several times at a disposable lighter, and finally exhaled smoke. He glanced at his wristwatch. His head moved back and forth as if he were nodding to himself.

The sound of shoes on gravel approached behind him, but the man did not turn around to look. Mixed in with the footsteps he could hear people talking. There were five of them, young men and women. It wasn't until they were some distance away that he gave them a glance to make sure.

Footsteps again, approaching. In the heart of a big city, many went out of their way to seek greenery, even on a weekday morning.

But this time the footsteps didn't pass him by. They arrived at the bench next to his, and there was merry laughter. A guy and a gal. The man took several puffs from his cigarette before he tossed it on the ground by his feet and stole a glance at the couple. After that, he lost interest in them.

"So I hear he's jealous now," the young man said.

The woman laughed.

"Like it wasn't too late," the youth continued. "He's dim. There's no point in him being jealous now."

"He's a hick."

"If all he was was jealous, it'd be funny."

"Oh, just let him say what he wants."

"But it pisses me off."

"He's just jealous."

There wasn't even a breeze. A calm, peaceful day. A few pigeons fluttered to the ground and shuffled their way over to where the man was sitting. They looked as though they were waiting for someone to throw them some food. The man hardly noticed them. The pigeons were tame, and they came right up to the man's shoes pecking around in the gravel for bugs.

"Tetsu, did you know Akiko's pregnant?" the gal asked.

"So it's true?"

"She threatened Yoshio, saying that she'll have it."

"That's scary. You'd never do that to me, would you?"

"We'll make sure I don't get pregnant, that's all."

"I'm doing my part."

"Akiko stopped taking the pill because it wasn't good for her skin."

"I never asked you to take it."

"I thought maybe you were hoping I would."

"Not if it messes up your skin."

A woman pushing a baby carriage passed behind them. Apparently the baby had just woken up, and the woman was making cooing noises at it.

Suddenly, someone was kicking at the gravel. The young couple turned their heads together toward the source of the sound. It was the man, who had kicked at the gravel with the toe of his shoe to scare the pigeons off, successfully. As a way of shooing pigeons, it was somewhat violent. But now he was staring quietly down at his feet.

After a couple of moments, the young couple got up.

They weren't laughing now. The huddled couple's footfalls trailed off along the gravel path.

The man lit a second Camel.

The pigeons he had scared away were regrouping, undaunted, by his feet. Apparently they got free food only around the benches. And right now the man was the only person around.

He merely watched the pigeons as they edged closer. He smoked peacefully, doing nothing to scare them away.

His cigarette was down to the butt. He flung it on the ground and crushed it with his shoe. He noticed then that one of the buttons was hanging loose from the sleeve of his jacket. He pinched the thread with his fingernails and tugged at it several times, then, clicking his tongue in disgust, ripped off the button. Playing for a while with it in his palm, he finally dropped it softly into the breast pocket of his jacket.

The man bent over forwards and offered his palms to the pigeons at his feet. They didn't come clucking to him. The man rose from the bench without straightening himself up. Still in a crouch, he put one foot forward stealthily. The pigeons scattered a little. Cautiously, he put another foot forward. Like a clumsy cat stalking a chosen prey.

He puckered his lips and made clucking noises. The pigeons, never taking to the air, just hopped a little farther away each time he took another step.

For a moment, the man stood up straight and quickly surveyed his surroundings. He had the air of a true wild beast for that brief moment.

He crouched down again. A step, then another. He was incredibly tenacious. Every time he reached out his hands, the pigeons hopped away.

A whole ten minutes had elapsed when he stretched his back for the second time.

Once again he examined his surroundings, like an animal. He looked more wary than ferocious. It was as though he needed to make sure no other animals were stalking him while he was busy hunting.

The man crouched again.

The pigeons were taking turns. A few would fly away, and another few would alight to take their place, perhaps to see whether feed had been scattered by someone.

The man seemed to have his eye on a particular pigeon. He showed no interest in the ones that came and went. He crouched lower and lower, until he was practically squatting.

The man's body stiffened. Split second. The tension left his shoulders. Hands, until then so cautious, now reached out casually. He grabbed the pigeon with both hands as though it were a stuffed animal.

He was quite a distance from the bench now. He walked back to it slowly.

He sat down. The first thing he did was not to look at the pigeon in his hands, but to glance around. Like a beast that had caught its prey.

The man loosened his tie a little more. The pigeon,

which was being held down against his lap with one hand, lay perfectly still. The man's free hand, the right, began to grope the body of his prey. Clouds of white fluff flew up from where his hand groped. He was pulling soft downy feathers from beneath the wings. Perhaps the pigeon was being held down skillfully; it showed no sign of trying to break free. Only, it kept shaking its head from right to left with a sort of desperation.

More feathers dropped to the ground than wafted through the air. After a while, it looked like light snow had fallen around the man's shoes.

The man looked up.

A young boy in shorts, five or six years old, stood staring at the man. Or rather, at what his hands held. His eyes on the boy, his fingers continued their work.

"These guys taste good roasted," the man said vacantly. For the first time, the boy looked up at the man's face.

"They serve birds at *yakitori* places. You gotta pluck their feathers out while they're alive, else it doesn't taste so good."

The expression on the boy's face didn't change. If the boy was frightened by what he saw, he didn't show it.

"Ever had *yakitori*, kid?"

The boy gave his head a faint shake.

"You will when you grow up. Don't forget, kid, those feathers need to be plucked while the bird's still alive. That's the way it is."

A woman's voice called out. The boy turned around.

The woman, who must have been the boy's mother, approached behind a baby carriage. The man didn't bother to look at her.

The boy ran off.

And now, as if he had suddenly lost interest in it, the man tossed up the pigeon. What seemed like a round object, when it was tossed up in the air, suddenly spread wings, as though the pigeon had forgotten about them and just remembered.

"Feathers. They'll grow back." It sounded like he was talking to someone, but the boy was already with his mother now, too far away to hear.

He stared over at the clump of trees again. He glanced down at his watch, and then directed his gaze back to the trees. He squinted into the sunlight. The wrinkles deepened around the corners of his eyes, and he looked much older than he did when he was relaxed.

His hands moved. His expression didn't change, but his eyes were fixed on one point, unmoving. He raised his hands to his tie and pulled the knot tight with his fingertips, his eyes still fixed ahead of him.

A fat man approached along the gravel path. The man's eyes seemed to follow him as he came closer. The man scratched at the feathers with his feet, and the white fluffy down was covered in dirt and gravel.

He didn't bother to get up, not even when the fat man stopped and stood beside him.

"Sit down. It's a nice day."

"In front of the museum!" the fat man said as he sat down. The walk seemed to have taken it out of him; he sounded slightly out of breath, and was dabbing constantly at his forehead with a handkerchief. "Why here?"

"Nice view. No cars. And I said noon 'cause there's more people around then."

"Being careful?"

"Yeah. I've been here an hour already."

"Why? What are you looking out for? Worried the cops might put in an appearance, Tanaka-san?"

"Territory. Look at those black ones over there. I meant the birds, not the humans. Crows. Well, that patch around by those trees is their territory. Just like this place here is the pigeons' territory."

"Yes, and?"

The fat man looked around fifty. Apart from the fact that he was starting to go thin on top, he looked more impressive than the man sitting next to him. His clothes were top-notch, too.

"Just so we understand each other, tell me it's just this once," the fat man said, taking out a white envelope from the inside pocket of his jacket.

"Understand each other? Understand what?"

"That this is the last time you're going to threaten me like this."

"Threaten you?"

The man took the white envelope and riffled the bills inside with his fingertips. The bills were crisp new ones that made a fluttering sound like playing cards being shuf-fled. He didn't bother counting them all. "I'm just doing my buddies a favor. Talking things over with you, collect-ing the compensation from you on their behalf. What's wrong with that?"

"On the surface, nothing." The fat man wrapped his handkerchief around his neck. He was still sweating. "The reason I agreed to talk to a pro like you is that I wanted to get this over and done with once and for all."

"You only get one chance at life."

"What do you mean by that?"

"Nothing. My philosophy, if you like. When you said 'once and for all,' I was reminded."

The pigeons were gathering around his feet again. He stared at them, but made no move to catch one this time.

"I've been patient, too, Tanaka-san. I kept quiet and paid up. Because I thought we had an agreement it would be just this once."

"Now it's getting in the way."

"Sorry?"

"That crow, see. It's on the pigeons' turf now. You can't eat that kind, though."

"Crows, you mean?"

"Now you, you're a human being. And people have their territories, too."

"Sometimes I don't understand what you're trying to say."

"Don't talk like you know me. It's only the third time

we met."

"That's more than enough for me." The fat man gave up trying to wipe the sweat from his face and looked irritably up at the sky. For all appearances, it was just the sunshine that was bothering him.

The man put a wrinkled Camel between his lips. The fat man watched the smoke coil up toward the sky.

"Nice day, huh?" the man said.

"Yes. As for me, though, I'd rather be in the shade."

"Why'd you wanna miss out on the sunshine?"

"Some things you just have to be in the mood for."

"Not feeling good?"

"What do you expect?"

"That's too bad." The man let out a laugh and the lines in his face deepened. "You like *yakitori*?"

"That's a strange question. Well, the doctor says I have to limit my intake of protein."

"Yeah? You diabetic?"

"And I've got high blood pressure. I'm not on a strict diet, though. Not like I've got that much time left anyway. You've got to allow yourself a few pleasures in life." The fat man laughed weakly.

More people were appearing on the hill. Several people were spreading out picnics. It was lunchtime.

"I don't get it."

"What?"

"People who don't know how to enjoy the sunshine."

"I know how. I'm just not in the mood right now."

"Just one chance, that's all you get. Here and now. Same for everyone. You just don't know how to enjoy yourself."

Smoke drifted up into the air again. The man paid it no attention. He wasn't looking down at the pigeons by his feet any longer, either. It was hard to tell what he was looking at. Silent and still, he sat on the bench with the envelope still in his hand.

"So it'll be just this once?"

"You won't get another day like this one."

"I want a straight answer."

"You'll never get another day like this."

"So this won't happen again—do I understand you right?"

The man ground out his cigarette and slid the envelope into the inner pocket of his jacket.

"Looks like that crow's taken off again. Must have come over just to try and stir shit up on the pigeons' territory."

"Who cares about the stupid crow?"

"It's important. We'll never see another day like this one." He threw down his cigarette and crushed it underfoot, extremely slowly. It was as though the sunshine had atrophied every muscle in his body.

"You've got a good thing going. I'm envious," the fat man said. He folded his handkerchief over and started dabbing away at his sweat.

"What, you starting to miss what's in the envelope?"

"Give me a break."

"I keep it, then."

The man looked up at the sky, only to lower his gaze again right away. He must have looked straight at the sun, because he screwed his eyes shut and stayed that way for a while.

"Feathers grow back."

"What are you talking about?"

"*Yakitori.*"

"A man should eat what he likes."

"You can't eat women, though."

"For God's sake." The fat man's lips curled into a smile.

"You can go now," Tanaka said, bending over and scooping up a handful of gravel. He scattered the gravel on the grass like bird seed. Ten or more birds flew over, but at least half of them flew straight away again when they saw they had been tricked.

"How long you planning on sitting here?"

"All right, I'm going. You want me to leave, right?" The fat man got up but made no move to leave. He was looking down at the man on the bench as if there was still something he had to say.

"Tell me this was one time only."

No answer. The fat man gave up and started to walk away. The shadow he cast on the gravel was round like a ball.

"Never look straight into the sun," the man muttered. "Nearly blinded me." No one was listening. He pressed the

palms of his hands against his eyes and rubbed them gently a couple of times. Then he took out another Camel and
lit it. The last one. He crumpled up the pack and threw it
on the grass. Once again, a flock of pigeons flew over to
investigate.

For the first time, the man seemed to follow the smoke
from his cigarette with his eyes, but he looked down again
as soon as his line of vision came too close to overlapping
with the direct rays of the sun.

He breathed out a stream of smoke and loosened his
tie, as if to let the sun's rays reach into his shirt and shine
warmth on his chest.

There were still four pigeons at his feet.

He stared down at one of them. For several minutes he
sat quite still, his eyes fixed on the ground in front of him.
Ash fell from the cigarette between his lips, but he didn't
seem to notice.

The pigeons moved about. The man followed one with
his eyes.

The heat finally reached his lips and he spat out his cigarette.

People's voices. Footfalls on the gravel path, now more
frequent. Lunch hour on a weekday afternoon. A fragment
of big city bustle carried into the park.

His gaze was still fixed on the pigeon. His body moved
slightly, as though to lift himself up from the bench. He
reached out a hand. He clucked twice.

That was all.

His gaze floated up toward the sky, but not to follow the pigeon, which remained by his feet.

He dug around in his pocket. No more cigarettes. Even so, he didn't stand up.

The sun was at its zenith.

# EIGHT YEARS

The man's gaze didn't leave the bartender's hands the whole time he was busy with his shaker. The bartender had his eyes closed. The lack of rattle and noise as he shook the ice-filled shaker spoke as eloquently of his years of experience as the lines around his eyes. All six customers at the counter were utterly caught up in the show.

He wasn't as old as he looked. The man looked up from the bartender's hands to his wrinkled face.

The bartender poured the contents of the shaker into two cocktail glasses. It was a green drink, clear, like cheap soda water. The bartender set the glasses down on the counter in front of a middle-aged couple.

"Not quite," the man said in a low voice.

The bartender shot him a blank look.

"You left the last swig in the bottom of the shaker. A real pro wouldn't have left a drop. Would have filled both glasses right to the top."

The bartender gave a vague nod. The background music was so quiet that the couple who ordered the cocktail must have heard him too.

"I like how you're nice and quiet with the ice, though."

The man was drinking beer. He'd been in for nearly an hour now but hadn't finished half the bottle.

"Your first time here, sir?"

"Nope."

"My cocktails happen to be a selling point."

"Sorry about that. All I meant to do was give you my two bits."

The man put a cigarette in his mouth, but the bartender made no move to light it for him. The snap of the man's lighter echoed through the bar. When he put it back down on the black marble counter, it sent an awkwardly loud clap through the place. A woman got up from the booth and walked over to where the man was sitting. She put her hand on his shoulder. She looked about thirty, and was dressed all in black.

The man gave his shoulders a shrug, and the woman took her hand away.

"You all right with beer, Tanaka-san?"

"Yeah, I like beer."

"But this one's gone flat. Here, let me get you another."

"No, this one's fine."

It was a small bar, with just one semi-circular booth and counter space. At most it would fit twelve, maybe thirteen people. A young woman was yapping away happily from inside the booth.

The bar itself was quite dark, but there was one bright light that shone straight down onto the counter. The man's beer looked sad and out of place in the glare, but he didn't seem to care. A gray suit and a dark tie. A man you might find anywhere. But the lines etched into his face were deeper even than the bartender's, and they made his age hard to guess.

The customer at the next stool ordered another cocktail. The bartender lowered his head and shot the man in the gray suit a look.

While pouring some ice and a shot from several different bottles into the shaker, the bartender stole a few glances at the man, but he was simply staring down at his beer, his expression utterly unreadable. The man was sitting at the far end of the counter, leaning with his right shoulder against the wall.

The bartender started mixing the drink. This time he didn't close his eyes. He shot the man a defiant look and poured the drink slowly into the glass. It was the color of peach flesh. He poured every last drop of liquid, until the glass was full to the brim. The liquid seemed to take on a life of its own in the glass.

The bartender looked over at the man, but the man's eyes were fixed on his own glass of beer.

"Are you sure there's nothing I can make for you sir?"

"I hate cocktails."

"It's all right, chief, Tanaka-san always has beer." It was the woman in black. She started chatting with the couple at the counter. The bartender joined in.

The threesome sitting in the booth got up. The two

girls went out to see off the man . It was already one in the morning.

"Would you mind calling us a cab?" Apparently the couple at the counter were thinking of calling it a night too. The bartender picked up the phone. "Me too," said the customer sitting next to the man.

The two girls came straight back. They implored the couple at the counter to stay for another drink, but it was clear from their tone of voice that they didn't mean it.

"Emi-chan, planning on having Yoshino-san take you home?" a woman's voice asked.

"Yeah! Let the Big Bad Wolf tuck you in," the customer sitting next to the man responded, laughing.

"Hmm, I might just let the wolf have me tonight." The young woman who said this was wearing a loud red dress with a plunging neckline. It looked cheap.

A pair of customers who had been drinking quietly at the counter got up before the taxis arrived. One of them was an elderly man and the other was about thirty. They were both wearing gray suits, as if they had arranged it beforehand. Something about their suits, however, was different from the one the man with the beer wore. No one would have noticed the color of his suit—it seemed such an integral part of him.

The girls saw the men off to the doorway and went to sit down at the counter.

"Yoshino-san is all talk. Once you get in the cab with him, he's a perfect gentleman."

"That depends on who I'm with."

The bartender started clearing off the counter. He was about to reach for the beer, but the woman stopped him with a slight shake of her head. Instead, he lifted the bottle and the glass and just wiped the counter.

The man lit up yet another cigarette. His ashtray still hadn't been emptied.

"You're supposed to look after all your customers, no matter who they are, buddy."

"I thought I'd take care of everything before we closed up."

"Some customers don't like it when you do that."

The bartender ignored him.

"Do men flirt even when they're in a cab on the way home to their wife and children?" the young woman in the red dress asked the customer called Yoshino.

"I'm telling you, it depends on the woman."

"I bet Yoshino-san never gets around to it."

The woman in black interceded, "Yoshino-san is the type who'd never toy with a woman he really liked, Emi-chan."

"Ah, that's how I should look at it," the young woman concluded.

The beer had gone flat. The man tossed his cigarette into his glass. The sizzling sound of the cigarette going out silenced the bar for a moment.

"I wonder if the cab isn't here already," the woman in black said.

The middle-aged couple got up.

"You're going too, Emi-chan." Rather than prompt Yoshino directly, the woman dressed in black prompted the girl. They all stood talking in the doorway for a while. The bartender was chatting pleasantly, saying goodnight.

The man leaned on the counter, putting his hand to his cheek. His tie was now loose around his neck.

The woman in black came back. "Thanks, chief, I'll deal with the rest," she said. The bartender didn't answer. He tried to clear away the man's beer.

"Drink it," the man said.

"What, with the cigarette butt in it?"

"It's good enough for the likes of you."

"Chief, why don't you go on ahead home?" the woman intervened.

"I still need to clean up. And there's still a customer here."

The man watched in silence as his beer bottle was cleared away. Someone had turned off the music as well. It was quiet enough to hear a pin drop.

"The lady just told you to go home. Didn't you hear her, buddy?"

"I'm not ready to leave yet."

"And you're not even drinking the cigarette beer."

"What does that have to do with anything?"

"Chief, really, it's all right," the woman said, apparently not overly concerned. She had lit a cigarette and was breathing out a lazy stream of smoke. The bartender quickly got out a clean ashtray.

"Go home, buddy."

"I told you I don't want to. Why don't you? It's not good business having people sitting around forever drinking just one beer."

"When you do what you need to do, I'll leave, too."

"Asking for a little pocket money or something?"

"No, your life."

"Real funny," the bartender retorted. He kept scrubbing the same spot on the counter.

"You scared?"

"Don't threaten me."

"Go home."

The woman blew a cloud of smoke in the air, annoyed. She looked classier when she wasn't talking than when she was chatting it up with the customers. The man lit a cigarette, and the woman pushed her ashtray in front of him. The bartender turned up the lights. Things lost their allure in the brightness. The flowers on the wall and the dark ceiling just looked grimy. Even the woman looked much older.

"He's a real bore, isn't he?" the man said, turning to the woman as he spoke. The woman just breathed out another stream of smoke.

"Go home, buddy," the man repeated. "I'm not going to cause any trouble."

"The customer should go home first."

"All right, I get it. Why don't we leave together, then?"

The bartender threw his rag down at the counter.

"Stop it." It wasn't clear to whom the woman was speaking.

The bartender leaped out from behind the counter. The man got off the stool with a half-smile of disbelief, and looked over at the woman. She kept on smoking.

The two went outside. The woman leaned on the counter, hand to cheek, and absent-mindedly let her gaze wander across the bottles of alcohol. She realized that the cigarette she was holding had gone down, and ground it out in the ashtray.

Her face reflected dimly in the black granite counter. She traced its outline with her finger over and over. Her expression didn't change.

She kept drawing on the countertop, but she seemed to have lost interest in the activity and merely pushed her finger around. She closed her eyes occasionally, like she couldn't stay awake.

Not much time had elapsed.

The door opened, and the man came back inside. He was fretting over a button hanging off his suit. He tried to yank it off, but gave up. He straightened his tie.

"He went home."

"Oh?"

"I don't have time to come over here every month. But that doesn't give you any reason to forget who owns this place."

"I haven't forgotten." She lit a cigarette.

The man put his elbows on the counter and stared at

the bottles behind the bar. His carefully combed hair was only slightly mussed. He put his hands on either side of his head, trying to smooth down his hair.

"He won't be showing his mug to anyone for a week. Around here, never."

"You think a woman like me can stay faithful when you come by only once a month? Sometimes just once every two months?"

"You tell me."

"You're terrible."

"I don't know. It's better this way. I choose to remain ignorant about certain things."

"Oh there's an excuse. Keeping me waiting."

"You're slow to catch on, aren't you? I can't tell it to you, get it? That's why I have to be ignorant with you."

The man saw his face reflected on the black surface. He started smoothing down his hair again. He eventually gave up and took a small comb out of his pocket. He was presentable again. The only difference was the dangling button.

"Gimme a whiskey."

"You're going to drink?"

"Just shut up and make me something."

"Don't drink, please. It's been so long."

"We're in a bar, aren't we?"

"But we're closed now. Anyway, I don't have anything good."

"If you're not going to give me anything, I'll get it

myself."

"You're trying to get back at me, aren't you? He was nothing. A man like you getting angry about a nobody."

"I'm the sort of man that drinks as much as I want when I want. I'd rather stay that way, that's all." He smiled faintly.

The woman shot up out of her seat.

She looked much more at ease standing behind the bar. She gave him a shot of scotch. He downed it in one swig.

The door opened and the bartender came in, his face streaming with blood. He had a knife in his right hand. He just stood there, the door wide open.

"Dammit! Get out of here!" the woman shouted. The bartender took a step into the room.

The man didn't even attempt to move. He merely glanced at the bartender and looked down sadly at his empty shot glass.

"Step out," the bartender said.

The man didn't budge. He didn't even look up. The bartender took another step in, but didn't come any closer.

"Get out of here, now! You idiot! Do you want to get killed?"

"I..."

"Whatever, just get out of here, now. Before you really piss him off."

The bartender started to speak. His lips moved, but nothing came out.

"Get the fuck out of here. Now!" the woman screamed.

The bartender shrank back two steps. He turned his back on them.

The door closed slowly.

"You must have lost your touch. I thought he wasn't supposed to come back."

"Yeah, well."

He was playing with the empty shot glass in the palm of his hand. The bottom of the glass hit the counter, making a tapping sound that was almost like footsteps.

"I felt sorry for him. When I was beating him up, I mean. I went soft."

"No, you just lost your touch."

"Maybe you're right."

"Why don't you give it up and just manage the bar? I think you'd have a lot more fun."

The man made the tapping sound on the counter again.

"You don't get it...what it is that makes a man happy in life."

"I don't even want to know."

The woman had already forgotten about the bartender. The man looked over at the door, as if to make sure he wouldn't come back. He made a tapping noise on the counter.

"Those young daredevils."

"He reminded me of you. Of when you were young. Didn't you see it, looking at him?"

"Maybe."

"You know, it's been eight years now, since I fell for you."

"Has it been that long?"

"Eight years. What a stupid little fool I used to be."

"Used to be. He'd have knifed me for sure if you hadn't gotten rid of him. There was nothing I could do except sit here."

The woman set out another shot glass on the counter and poured a whiskey. He reached out for it. She pushed his hand away and drank it herself.

"I'd like one, too," the man said.

"No way, you'd still be of some use right now. After another, you'll be useless."

"Use, eh?" He laughed faintly. She seemed to sense what he meant by that laugh. She didn't bolt away this time.

"You got to know when your time's up," she said. "Everyone's got an expiration date."

"Not men."

"There'll be others coming at you with knives. And someday, one of them will stab you."

"Thanks for that." He made the tapping sound on the counter again. The woman tightened her grip on her half-full glass.

"I've been knifed lots of times already. I made it this far."

"Don't be so sure you'll get away with it forever."

"Don't sound so cocksure yourself."

"I just don't buy it that all men are is strong."

He laughed again. She didn't move a muscle. He got out a cigarette and she offered him a light.

The smoke he breathed out lingered between them before dissipating. The lighting in the bar was bright enough to trace the movement of the smoke.

"I'm going to close things up."

"So?"

"So you're going to escort me home. It's decided."

"Decided?"

"Yes. You're going to romance me again, like you did eight years ago."

"Ah, women." He made the same tapping sound on the counter again. She brought the glass to her lips. She poured the remaining third of it into his glass. He watched her silently.

"I think you'd still be okay. It's after you've had two that you're no good."

"You turned out all right, sweetheart."

"Eight years is a long time."

He didn't touch the whiskey, but kept tapping on the counter.

# HOURGLASS

It was bright outside.

The man was sitting on the sofa, staring at the wall vacantly. A short-sleeve undershirt and pants that needed ironing. He wasn't wearing any socks. He reached out for a cigarette suddenly and lit it with the desk lighter on the table. Two, three rings of smoke drifted from his mouth. Smoke rose from the ashtray. Eventually other butts got lit too and the smoke intensified.

He stared at it for a while. He had the same expression on his face as when he had been staring at the wall. More smoke. A plain glass ashtray. There were a lot of cigarette butts.

The man got up, clicking his tongue in annoyance. He came back with a glass half-filled with water. He poured it all into the ashtray. It made a sizzling sound. The water spread out to the edges of the ashtray, and some of the butts floated to the top.

"Guess that's it," he muttered. He reached over for another cigarette. "They suck up water and settle at the bottom."

He stared at the ashtray, not moving from his place on

the sofa. The floating water-logged cigarette butts sank and bounced off the butts already at the bottom. The expression of satisfaction on the man's face lasted only for a moment. He turned his gaze back to the wall, as if deep in thought. He didn't notice the ashes dropping on the carpet. The cigarette butts sucked up most of the water in the ashtray. The man stuck his cigarette in the middle of the bunch.

"Too little water, and they don't go out," he muttered again. He didn't seem to realize he had spoken out loud.

He got up and walked over to the window. He stared at a water supply tank on the roof of a building somewhere far off in the distance.

The phone rang.

It was on the sideboard, which was right up against the wall. He stared at the phone for some time. It rang five times before he walked over to it slowly and picked it up.

"Tanaka here," he said. He held the receiver against his ear for a while without speaking. He placed a hand on the edge of the sideboard. It was level with his stomach. He scratched at its surface repeatedly with his forefinger. Like he was trying to get rid of grime.

Then he said, "Don't." His finger stopped moving.

"I heard you. Stop repeating yourself, will you? Things don't flare up so easily, okay? If we start rushing things, they will too." He glanced out the window. It was light out. He straightened out the dark blue cloth under the phone.

"Even if something's up, nothing's happening till dark.

Stop panicking."

He opened the glass door of the sideboard. He took out a small hourglass. He stared at the falling white sand as he held it. Before all the sand could reach the bottom, he turned it over.

"I'm coming, but I can't get there right away, got it? I need to take care of some things first. I probably won't get there till after dark."

He turned the hourglass over again.

"You don't have to tell me that."

Now he was pressing the receiver less tightly to his ear.

"Let me guess, the Boss isn't there, is he? He's probably hiding somewhere, with some protection. So there's no reason to panic. Five guys is more than enough."

He tapped the hourglass against the sideboard. The sand stopped when the hourglass hit the sideboard, and then started falling again. It fell more slowly than when he left it alone.

"I got it. I got it," he spat out. He hung up. He stood there for a while, staring at the hourglass.

He shook his head a couple of times, and left the room. He came back holding a white basket. He cut across the room and went out on to the balcony.

He began hanging up his laundry. He took one item out at a time, straightening out the wrinkles, shaking out the water, and then pegging it on the line. Four undershirts. Six boxer shorts. Four towels. And some socks.

The newspaper on the table started rustling from the

breeze blowing in through the balcony door. He walked back in with the empty basket. He shut the door and the newspaper stopped rustling.

He sat down on the sofa. As if he'd finished some big job, he reached for a cigarette, put it in his mouth, and lit up ceremoniously. He left the basket at his feet.

He moved his lips several times. No words came out. He didn't move from his seat, even after he had finished his cigarette. He was expressionless.

He picked up the newspaper. He flipped through it, not really interested in its contents, and folded it up in four before tossing it onto the magazine rack. He pulled up the cuff of his pants and scratched at his calf. His leg didn't have much hair on it and was chalky white compared to his face and hands. But the area he was scratching soon turned red. He kept scratching. It got redder. He smeared some saliva on it.

He put another cigarette in his mouth. He didn't light it right away. He watched the laundry outside the window, fluttering in the breeze.

The phone rang.

"Tanaka here." He was holding the unlit cigarette. "I'm aware of that. Please don't worry." He twisted his face as if in pain. "It's nothing. We can take care of it on our own. Just stay where you are, please. It'll be a piece of cake."

The muscles in his face kept twitching as he spoke. His eyes glinted with hatred from time to time, contrary to his polite language.

"It's better for us to be patient now and see what happens. If we start mobilizing, it could end up working against us. I know what I'm doing. I'm not an amateur."

He was still holding the cigarette. He tore it lengthwise in two.

"You've let me run things my way so far, so times like this I feel I ought to do my best for you. In any case, please stay where you are and relax, and things will turn out fine." He went on tearing the cigarette into thin strips. Tobacco leaves and white bits of paper fluttered onto the sideboard.

"I know. Depending on the situation, I'll negotiate with them. In any case, please stay where you are. You'll be fine with five young guys there. Just make sure those five don't go anywhere."

After he hung up, he started muttering under his breath. It went on for a while. He swept the debris on the sideboard into the palm of his hand.

He went back to the sofa, got another cigarette and lit up. He blew out a few clouds of smoke and threw the cigarette violently into the ashtray. He got up, picked up the phone, and dialed.

"It's me, Tanaka." He slammed down on the sideboard with his fist. All the sand had dropped to the bottom of the hourglass. It shook slightly from the vibration.

"What, you still home? Cut the shit or I'll beat the crap out of you. You're supposed to be there until I can get there. I'm on my way. I'm trying to finish up over here so I can get there, you hear? Idiot. I'll be there in a few hours. You be there in half an hour. Got it? You better be there in half an hour." He threw down the phone and threw himself down on the sofa.

He seemed distracted. After a good while, he slowly rolled up the other leg of his pants this time. There was a scab on his shin. He started scratching away, but didn't scratch for as long. He suddenly jolted up and started clearing away the things that were lying around the room.

He picked up the magazines, flew out of the room to get a rag, and wiped down the table and the sideboard with quick, brisk movements. He even wiped the little hourglass with great care, holding it pinched between his fingers.

It didn't take long. The room wasn't exactly a mess to begin with. Finally, he went out to empty the ashtray and wiped it clean, too.

The phone rang.

He glanced over at the clock on the wall.

"Tanaka here." He was holding the dirty rag in his right hand. He threw it on the table.

"Kawano's not there yet?" He shook his head a couple of times. "The plan was that Kawano'd be there until I could get there. He should be there soon. I'm going to be a little late. Don't panic, I'm telling you! Kawano should get there soon. After that, just wait for me. Don't go doing anything stupid, got it? The fact that they aren't there yet says they don't know what's up either."

He dialed a number as soon as he hung up.

"You're on your way?"

He kicked the sideboard. The glasses inside the case shook.

"Didn't you hear what I said? Thirty minutes. Didn't I say that? It's been thirty minutes already. You're a bigger idiot than I thought. I'm not asking for excuses. I'm done here now and I'm coming. If you're not at the office when I get there, you're dead."

He kicked the sideboard again. One of the glasses fell over. He gently opened the sideboard door and reached in with his hand. He found the glass and righted it.

"I'm not saying one more word, Kawano. See you there."

He hung up.

He left the room and came back after a moment, carrying two plastic bags.

He put them on the table, staring at them absently. There was something wrapped in a white cloth inside one of them. He took it out carefully and unwrapped it.

It was a short-barreled gun. He checked out the gun chamber, spinning it a few times, and aimed it. He cocked the hammer and put it back.

"Damn idiot," he muttered. He started polishing the gun with a white rag. He stopped for a cigarette and then went on polishing.

The phone again.

"Tanaka here."

The gun lay on the cloth on the table.

"The Boss's worried?" He was tapping the sideboard with his fingertips. His other hand took the receiver now and then.

"How many are you now?" He put his palm down flat on the sideboard. He rotated his palm to make squeaky noises, again and again.

"That should be enough, since the Boss isn't there. We need the others to watch over him. If you run around like idiots, we'll seem scared as shit. It's not enough just to have the numbers."

He finally took his hand away from the sideboard. He began to scratch at his hair.

"Kawano there yet? No? What's he doing, that idiot? If he can't take care of things when I'm not there, he's useless. He was supposed to get there right away. He ought to know what he's supposed to do."

His fingertips started tapping the sideboard again.

"I know. Nothing's happened since, right? Just listen to me and things'll be fine. I'm not finished here yet. If anything's going to happen, it'll be after dark. Not while it's light out. Hey, listen to me. That's how it is. It's too risky in daylight, for both sides. That's why it's going to be after dark. I'm telling you, it'll be night. I'm right on this one, trust me."

He hung up.

"Damn cowards," he spat out.

He sat down on the sofa, throwing out his legs, and smoked a cigarette. There was only one cigarette in the ashtray.

He smoked down a second to the filter before he finally put it out.

He resumed polishing the gun. He blew at it from time to time, to get rid of the dust. He flipped out the chamber and flipped it back. It made a metallic clink. His head to one side, he repeated the motion over and over.

He looked over at the clock. He placed the gun gently on the white cloth, as if it were a fragile object.

He reached for the phone.

He dialed a number and waited a while before hanging up.

"He's just wandering around," he said articulately, but to no one. "He's killing time, that idiot." He returned to polishing the gun.

He stopped in the middle of polishing and left the room. The faint sound of running water.

He was barechested when he came back into the room. A deep gash ran across his shoulder blade. It looked like an old wound. There were no other scars. He got out a white dress shirt from the dresser in the corner of the room. It was still covered in plastic from the dry cleaners. He put it on over his bare torso and threw on his tie. A dark, understated tie. Facing the mirror, he readjusted it and ran a comb through his hair.

He changed to a pair of trousers. The spot where he had scratched himself on his calf had turned a bright red color, like a bruise. He pulled on his socks and fastened his belt.

He said to himself again: "The asshole's just killing time."

He sat down on the sofa, staring at the gun for some time. He picked it up once and then put it back on the table.

"Gotta teach him a lesson one of these days." He adjusted his tie.

He got up and reached for the phone. He started dialing, hesitated for a moment, then dialed the rest.

"Hey, it's me." He wound the cord around a finger, in an almost feminine gesture.

"I gotta go out." The cord unwound. "It's a pain in the ass. We might get into a dispute. The Boss ran off. He's hiding out somewhere, pissing his pants. He couldn't lead a fight even if he wanted to. He's just a fucking geezer now."

He reached for the hourglass. He turned it over. The sand began to trickle down.

"One of the kids got stabbed, that's all. Wasn't a good situation to start off with. Might be enough to set things off."

He watched the sand.

"He told me to man the office. Who's he fucking kidding? Can't expect us to sit around when we could get shot at any moment. That was the call. Keeps calling about it. Says he leaves it in my hands."

A quarter of the sand reached the bottom of the hourglass. He didn't touch it.

"I should go. I've been running things my way till now.

The Boss won't have any more of it. Blow him off now, and I'll never hear the end of it."

He started to reach for the hourglass, but then pulled back his hand.

"Goddamn warfare, at my age. If something goes wrong and I get caught, I won't get out for a year or two. Whatever, gotta deal with it." He wrapped the cord around his finger again. The bottom of the hourglass was a third full now. It wasn't a real hourglass; it was small, more of a toy.

"The fucking gall of my brother Kawano, after all I did for him. At a time like this too. He's freaking out." He closed his eyes and heaved a sigh. He didn't say anything for a while. He shook his head like he was sick of the whole thing.

"Shut up, woman, you don't understand a thing. I'm heading over to your place. I want you to keep my gun. After that, call the cops. With cops at the entrance, they can't do anything. I'll go to the office after the cops get there. It's better that way."

He hung up.

He looked out the window. It was still light out. He approached the table, and loaded the gun. There were only five bullets.

He looked in the barrel, as if to confirm it, and then casually dropped it in his pocket.

He stood for a moment glaring at himself in the mirror on his dresser door.

He put on his jacket and shut the dresser door.

But he didn't leave right away. He sat on the sofa, lit another cigarette, and smoked it slowly. When he put it out, he crossed his arms and sat thinking.

The hourglass had run out a while ago.

He got up, turned it over, and went out, shaking his head a little.

# PROFILE

The doorbell rang repeatedly.

The two young men looked at each other. The small, six-mat room didn't even have a table. There was only a small dresser and a huge TV set that looked out of place. A tired old curtain covered the aluminum-frame window.

One of the young men, a skinhead, threw a questioning look at the other. The bell kept ringing. The other one, who was thin and had a perm, jerked his chin toward the door.

"How 'bout we make a run for it?" the skinhead said. The perm just shook his head doubtfully.

"We're on the first floor," the skinhead urged. "Run fast enough, and we could shake 'em off."

"Could be just what they're waiting for. And they don't know nothing. No way they'd know. We just got to play dumb, is all."

"Maybe some asshole talked?"

"No use thinking about it now. Don't worry about it. Act like there's nothing going on. C'mon, we don't even know who's here."

They were talking in whispers. The sound of the television drowned out their words. Live horse racing.

The skinhead stood up, resigned. The perm reached over to turn up the volume. He was missing the top two joints of his little finger.

"Who's in there?" came a voice from the doorway. "Hurry up and open the door. Yoshimoto, you in there? Hey, Yoshimoto!"

The perm jumped up and shouted a reply.

"Goddamn, what a mess." A middle-aged man walked into the room. Curtains were nailed up all over the kitchen area. "And it fucking stinks. Clean up that mess in the sink."

Yoshimoto offered him the only cushion in the place. It was dirty.

"You're alone, Brother Tanaka?"

"You think I'd bring a lady here?" The man he'd called Tanaka sat down on the cushion, mindful of his pants. He reached for the phone. It was an old-fashioned one with a dial.

"It's Tanaka. The Boss there?"

Yoshimoto and the skinhead exchanged anxious glances. Tanaka lit a cigarette, still holding the phone. Yoshimoto quickly struck his lighter. He moved too fast and the light went out as he offered it to Tanaka. He hurriedly struck it again. It finally lit. Tanaka puffed out a stream of smoke in irritation.

"Ah ha. Then who's there?" Tanaka moved to flick the ashes off his cigarette. Yoshimoto offered him an ashtray.

"I'm at Yoshimoto's." He took a couple more puffs of his cigarette before tossing it in the ashtray. Yoshimoto put it out carefully.

"I know. I just wanted to make sure the Boss's all right. Yeah, I said I know. There's nothing you can tell me I don't already know. So the Boss's safe. I just had to deal with two hit men. Yeah, they came for me. I got enough on my hands over here, just trying to stay alive. It's a fucking embarrassment. There's one other kid over here. I was thinking we could do it just the three of us." He shook his head a little. Then, as if suddenly reminded of the fact that he was wearing a tie, he loosened it and then put another cigarette in his mouth. This time, Yoshimoto's light didn't go out.

"What 'take it easy'? They tried to kill me. If you think we can't do it just the three of us, send me another. I'm not going to just let it go. Those urchins hang out on enemy turf, and I'm just not going to let it pass." Tanaka moved to flick the ash off his cigarette, and Yoshimoto was already waiting with the ashtray. The skinhead was sitting in formal *seiza* style in the kitchen area.

"That so?" Tanaka threw the second cigarette into the ashtray. Again, Yoshimoto put it out carefully. Tanaka's teeth marks were on the filter.

"I got it. That's fine. Won't do nothin'. Go on, talk." On the cushion, Tanaka crossed his legs Indian-style, his left hand pressing the receiver to his ear, his right hand pulling at a crease in the *tatami* mat. He grunted a few times in response, but didn't utter any words.

The tatami began to rip where he scratched at it, but it was already torn in several different areas. Yoshimoto started doing it, too.

"Yeah, that's good. Let's do that. Can't do it alone. My shoulder's gone. It happened when I ducked the knife. Can't move my right arm." Tanaka, with the receiver still against his ear, stretched out his right arm and pushed the button to hang up the phone.

He threw down the receiver and stared back and forth between the skinhead and Yoshimoto. The skinhead was the first to start looking uncomfortable.

"What's this one's name?"

"It's Kajita. I was planning to introduce him to you one of these days, Tanaka Brother."

"He one of your little brothers, Yoshimoto?"

"Yes. He's no wimp—I thought he'd be good for the gang."

"Good timing. The Boss's been asking for more troops."

"I'm honored to meet you. I'll do my best." Kneeling in the kitchen area, Kajita put his hands on the floor and bent his head down low. Tanaka grunted at him and turned his gaze on Yoshimoto.

"You got a gun?"

"No. I did, until recently, but when they rounded them up for the office, I gave mine in."

"What about a knife?"

"I only have one of those wooden swords. That, I didn't

think I had to hand in."

"Go get it."

"Hey, you," Yoshimoto called to Kajita. Kajita got up and came back with the wooden sword right away. He handed it to Yoshimoto. Tanaka took it and brandished it once before putting it down beside him.

"Is your arm all right, Tanaka Brother?"

"I just made that up. They were afraid I'd act on my own, do something."

"Are you going there?"

"You two want to come along? If you're going to come, it means going for the enemy headquarters. It'll be tough without firearms."

"It's our first war."

"That's why it's a good opportunity for you two. But, I guess three won't be enough. Sooner or later, though, we'll have to have a chat with them. Try to be useful then."

Yoshimoto and Kajita bowed their heads slightly at the same time, as if nodding in assent. Tanaka got out his third cigarette. Yoshimoto got out his light right away.

"Being a *yakuza* isn't just about paying your dues or losing a finger, Yoshimoto."

"I get it."

"No, you don't. I've been in this world for more than twenty years and I still don't get it. The longer I stay alive, the more I see that I don't get it." Tanaka smoked his cigarette down to the filter. He put it out himself.

"You got any beer?"

Kajita sprang up. He put a glass in front of Tanaka and brought out an opened bottle of beer. Tanaka eyed Kajita's hands.

"Wait. Is it cold?"

"Not really. The fridge is old. It don't work right. Should I go buy some beer?"

"Nah, that'll do."

Kajita poured the beer. Half of it was head. He waited for the foam to rest and then poured a little more.

Three men walked in. They didn't bother ringing the doorbell or knocking. They still had their shoes on.

Tanaka's wooden sword suddenly came down on Kajita's shoulder. Kajita grabbed his shoulder and doubled over with pain. Yoshimoto lurched back, and barely propped himself up with his hands on the floor behind him. He opened his mouth as if to speak.

"No use pretending, Yoshimoto." Tanaka's voice was much lower than before. "Seems you two were planning to go over to their side. That was damn nice of you."

"Brother, I…"

"Yeah, I know what you were trying to do. You were only making it *look* like you were going to betray us, but really you were planning to double-cross them, right? How thoughtful of you, keeping your folks' interests at heart. Can't blame you for trying."

Tanaka got out another cigarette. One of the three guys who barged in offered him a light. Two of them were young, and the third was around Tanaka's age.

"Well, they figured out what you were up to. They found out that you were just *pretending* to betray us, so you could spy on their clan. They can't wait to throw you to the wolves. Oh no, I can't send you into that."

"I'm sorry, Tanaka Brother." Yoshimoto was shaking with fear.

"And you guys, were you in such a hurry you couldn't even take off your shoes?" Tanaka said, turning to the three with a laugh. The wrinkles about his eyes and around his mouth deepened when he laughed. "How many guys have you got outside?"

"Four."

"Hand over the skinhead."

"Wait!" Kajita shouted, still holding his shoulder. He was grabbed from both sides and pulled up to his feet.

"So long, kid. Sorry we had to meet this way."

"Wait! I'm begging you. Please, wait!" A dark stain spread over Kajita's crotch. He was dragged away. Voices came from outside the door.

"Where are they taking him?" Yoshimoto asked, his voice trembling. Tanaka lit a cigarette by himself and slowly breathed out a stream of smoke.

"The only place for traitors."

"Traitors?"

"Oh, you're different. You were just faking it, I know, for the gang."

"But I—"

"Don't mention it, Yoshimoto."

The two guys who dragged Kajita away came back in, this time taking off their shoes. The middle-aged man took off his shoes, too, lined them up, and sat down. The four of them were surrounding Yoshimoto, sitting *seiza*-style.

"Didn't I tell you being a *yakuza* isn't just about losing fingers, Yoshimoto? When they find out that you're in great health, while Kajita became fish food, they'll be pissed. What I'm saying is, you better watch your back from now on."

"Wait a minute, Tanaka Brother."

"Some scores can't be settled by losing a finger."

"What should I do then?"

"Take out Ohkawa."

"O...Ohkawa?" Yoshimoto turned pale.

"You do that, and you'll be an officer. No one'll complain about a punk like Kajita. You ought to be ready to do some time anyway."

"And if I don't want to?"

"No one's forcing you. But they'll be out for revenge. Info is always leaking between us and them; it'll be easy to make them think you went over there to spy on them." Tanaka tightened his tie. The other three were staring down at the tatami.

"We won't do anything to you. It's better for us that way. Right now, we're fifty-fifty with them. You get rid of Ohkawa, and we'll be winning seventy-thirty."

"But—"

"That's what being a *yakuza*'s all about, Yoshimoto." Now that he'd adjusted his tie, Tanaka looked forbidding again. He put a cigarette in his mouth. Yoshimoto wasn't the one who offered him a light.

Beads of cold sweat had broken out all over Yoshimoto's pale face. Tanaka stared at him, and breathed out a stream of smoke.

"What's going to happen to Kajita?"

"He wasn't really a member. He's no use to us dead or alive. But if he dies, they'll come after you for sure."

No one spoke for a while. The late afternoon sun came streaming in through the window.

After a long time, Yoshimoto gave an emphatic nod, ashen.

"Good, now get out of here. You're on stand-by."

The two young men got up and urged Yoshimoto up. Yoshimoto looked over at Tanaka and bowed his head before he stood up.

"To think I escaped the hit men, just to run in *here*."

The other man smiled. Tanaka started picking at the fold in the tatami. "I broke into a cold sweat when you told me on the phone."

"Well, they hadn't betrayed us yet. If they had, they wouldn't have let you in."

"But Yoshimoto?"

"He was asking us to give him a break for some time now—you know, about his share. That kind of fellow wouldn't be happy no matter where he goes—he wouldn't be any good anywhere."

"Wonder what they promised him."

"The usual stuff, I think—just to trick him and use him. Exactly the sort of thing we do."

"Maybe Yoshimoto thought there's some honest 'head-hunting' among *yakuza* too."

"He's only a kid, I suppose."

They both put a cigarette in their mouths at the same time. Facing each other, they lit their own cigarettes.

"So what was up with the hit men?"

"They only had knives, so I managed. I didn't think they'd come after me in the middle of the day. I didn't have any guys with me."

"You always did insist on going alone, whenever you went to see your lady friends."

"I was lucky. If he'd been packing heat, I would've taken a shot for sure."

"Better make sure Yoshimoto takes a gun."

"We'll give him a loaded one and let him loose." Tanaka put out his cigarette first. "And the Boss?"

"At the usual place, surrounded by ten of our junior members. He'll live it up with the ladies 'til we strike a deal. Same as usual."

"Nice work if you can get it."

"That's why he's at the top. Because he's a goddam coward."

"We have a hit man now, you know. Got to take advantage of him."

"They sent one over, and you send one over. You'll have something to coax the others with."

"Stick with me. I won't do you wrong. The Boss's only got another couple of years at most. Start saving, and you can retire when he croaks."

"I think I'm beginning to understand why the Boss don't want to die just yet."

"Fucking war, at a time like this." Tanaka began tearing at the tatami again.

"I'm going on ahead. Got to let the gang at the office know they sent you hit men."

"I owe you one. Thanks for letting me know Yoshimoto was a traitor."

"I told you 'cause it was you. Anyway, I know you'll pay me back."

"Until Yoshimoto makes a move, the story is that Kajita's fish food. Just leave it at that. We'll figure out what to do with Kajita later."

The other man nodded.

"It sucks," Tanaka dropped.

"What does?"

"This life."

"You only got a couple of years to go. There's no mistaking that you'll be boss next. Make it that way in the next couple of years."

"A couple more years, huh."

"Don't do anything that'll land you in prison."

"I've done enough time already, miserable time."

"You'll earn your medals in this war. And the junior members will follow you."

"To do that, I got to knock someone off."

"Ohkawa."

"Yeah."

The middle-aged man grabbed his shoes and stood up.

When Tanaka was alone again, he picked up the phone. "Gimme the Boss. It's Tanaka."

He sat there tearing at the tatami for a while as he waited.

"They sent me hit men. No, I'm fine. I'll take care of everything here. It's really nothing." He kept picking at the tatami with his right hand. The frays cast tiny shadows.

"I understand. I'll just knock off one of their junior leaders before we clash head on. We'll dominate them." Tanaka had broken out in a sweat, but it wasn't from the heat. He casually wiped his forehead with the palm of his right hand.

"Boss, I don't want you to have to get involved in this. May I please handle this war?" Tanaka grimaced. "All right. No, it won't take very long."

He put down the receiver and clicked his tongue in irritation. Then he spat on the tatami.

"Doesn't even know how to die," Tanaka muttered. "Can't even get it up anymore." He went for the tatami again but stopped after he picked at it a few more times. He looked pensive. Sunlight streamed in through the window, illuminating his profile.

# TABLECLOTH

A plate of *foie gras* sat on the table. It was covered in a rich sauce and surrounded by just a few red and green vegetables.

The man seemed unsure of which fork and knife to use. The elderly man sitting across from him reached out for his unhesitatingly. Taking the cue, the man picked up a fork first, then a knife.

"You know, Tanaka, *foie gras*..." the older man started to intone. He had graying hair and a ruddy complexion. A young waiter came in and carefully poured out the wine. Tanaka's glass first. There was a reddish residue in the bottom of the older man's glass, perhaps from when he had tasted the wine.

"This stuff's no good for an old man like me. But I just can't give it up. When I was a lot younger I tried to wash my hands of this whole business, but I couldn't get away from it. Same with *foie gras*."

"I never eat this stuff."

"You'll get hooked on it too. Some insist on having it with a sweet white wine. Ha, what do they know. It's got to be a full-bodied red."

"I don't know about wine. If it's booze, you drink it. That's all I know."

"This stuff, Chateau Margaux, sets you back forty-thousand yen."

"Forty-thou?"

The man brought his glass to his lips and took a sip. He closed his eyes for a moment and put the glass back on the table. He looked at the older man. "Boss, this isn't my kind of drink."

"So you do care about wine."

"Nah, what I meant is, I'd be just as happy knocking back cheap sake at the local stall. Stuff's lost on me."

"I was like that once." The older man swallowed the wine slowly. He had a big knotted scar on his neck, and each time he swallowed, it looked as if he were gulping down a bug. He had a bite of bread and another swallow of wine.

"You know why you have bread when you drink wine?"

"'Cause you're hungry."

"No, it clears your palate. That way you can taste the wine better."

"Is that right."

"Of course, that isn't the sort of thing a *yakuza* needs to know."

"That's what I think."

"So Tanaka, how many years have you served so far?"

"Must be eight years, if you add it all up. I went in four

times."

"Had enough, did you?"

"I was ready to go again, if I had to, what with the skirmishes that were going on."

"Well, thanks to you, we came to an understanding, and everything worked out. Two of our junior members'll be doing time, but no one got killed. Total victory. It's already easing our everyday operations."

"If you lose, in our business it means you're dead." The man stabbed at a slice of *foie gras* and put it in his mouth. He didn't seem to like it very much. He grimaced slightly. The older man, meanwhile, closed his eyes in ecstasy at each mouthful.

From the waist up, the man looked calm and relaxed, but underneath the table, he kept jiggling his knee. His polished shoes glinted in the light.

"Start getting used to this kind of life."

"I still got work to do, Boss. I can still be of use."

"Idiot. Of course I still need you to work for me. Just not in the capacity you're used to, but higher up."

"I'll go wherever you say."

"I want you to get together a gang of your own."

"Is that what we're here to discuss?"

"Yes." The older man had another sip of wine. There was only a small amount left in his glass.

"Hey," he called. A young man with a perm rushed in. "Not you! Send in the waiter."

The waiter heard this and hurried in.

"Quit shaking. When you shake the bottle, you stir up the dregs at the bottom."

The waiter's hand was trembling. He stood up straight and swallowed hard. He poured the wine again. The man emptied his glass.

"It's about time we put together another gang." The older man wiped his mouth with the napkin and started on the *foie gras* again. He sipped at the wine from time to time.

There was silence. The light over the table illuminated an ornately decorated room. The plate that held the *foie gras* was no less ornate, but the older man seemed indifferent to all but the delicacy itself.

They finished their plates in silence. The older man had had four glasses of wine.

"Tanaka, say yes. Time for you to step up."

"I'm not cut out for that stuff."

"You're the only one for the job. Got it? Several guys already answer directly to you. I let it go, in anticipation of today. Good food, good liquor, good cars, good women— all that's part of moving up in our world."

The man watched the dishes being cleared away. The older man put a cigarette in his mouth. Tanaka quickly offered him a light.

"My mind's made up, got it?"

The man stared at the empty plate. He was still jiggling his knee. It hadn't stopped the whole time they were talking.

There was a knock on the door. It wasn't the waiter. The young man with the perm came in with a cordless phone.

"For you. From Shimura *sensei*."

"Oh, hello, hello, this is Ohmura." The older man threw down his napkin. "Yes, of course. We don't rely on the dough from your connections." He picked up the napkin and crumpled it in his hand. Although he uttered words of assent, he squeezed the napkin repeatedly. From time to time, his fingernails turned white from the pressure of his grip.

"On our part, we have to make sure our guys don't go hungry. Several hundred guys, *sensei*. No wonder we require your assistance now and then. I thought all along that ours was a give-and-take relationship, but now when it's my back that's itching...."

His dinner partner was still looking down at the table, jiggling his knee. The older man's voice was much louder when he spoke on the phone.

"I promise we won't be unreasonable. It's almost election time, and the newspapers are bound to start hounding you. I've been told that getting elected costs a fortune, and that's why I'm not going to insist. Elections are serious stuff." He threw the napkin back down on the table.

"So we're still seeing each other this evening?" the older man said into the phone. He finished off his glass of water in one gulp as he listened, a bug squirming down his throat.

"Yes, *sensei*, damn diabetes and high blood pressure.

I'm falling apart."

"Boss—" the man said, but the older man held up his hand to silence him.

"No, I won't be having anything to eat. I'm on a diet."

He then threw the phone at the lackey with the perm.

"Damn politicians. Have to be careful, or they'll make us look like saints. You've got to draw the line and make sure they know it. You can't make any mistakes when you're dealing with politicians, Tanaka. Use them well, and they're a great asset."

He had gotten up even as he spoke.

Alone now, the man put his hand on the table and started pinching the tablecloth with his fingernails.

"Fucking die in a ditch, dotard." It was a faint mutter. "I'll spit on your face when you're dead." The invectives came streaming out of his mouth, but never too loud. He just gripped the tablecloth tighter.

He heard voices just outside the door. He quickly straightened out the tablecloth.

The door opened, and the older man came back in.

"Tanaka, I have to meet with Representative Shimura now. You're on your own for dessert and the rest. If you get lonely, call in one of your guys so he can have some liqueur too."

"Aye aye, sir," the man said and started heading for the door. The older man put out a hand to stop him.

"You don't have to see me off. You're a boss too now. Got it, Tanaka? And ask for the cognac. In fact, I'll tell the waiter which one to bring you."

Tanaka bowed his head. He stayed like that for a few moments, even after the door shut.

He went and sat at the table. He took his glass of water and splashed the water at the old man's seat. The table-cloth was splashed as well as the chair.

"Stuff yourself with good food, bastard. Fucking hide out with your women."

He sat in his seat for a while, muttering unintelligibly. He called out toward the door. The waiter came in.

"Tell one of the kids to come in. Oh, and the Boss spilled his water."

"I'll take care of it right away."

The waiter hesitated for a moment, not knowing which to do first. He came back with a young man all dressed up in a suit. The waiter had decided to take care of both tasks at the same time; he also removed the tablecloth and replaced the chair.

The man took out a cigarette, and the young man held out a light.

"Want a drink?" The words came out of his mouth together with a puff of smoke.

"Anything for me."

"Well, I'm having cognac. You have some, too."

"Um, sir, dessert is waiting to be served," the waiter said.

"Make it for two. He'll have the other one."

The waiter bowed low. He spread out a new tablecloth

before he left the room.

"The Boss always gets a private room in some classy restaurant when he's about to tell you something you don't wanna hear. Like anyone was ever intimidated by any of this crap." He'd stopped jiggling his knee.

"What did the Boss tell you?"

"Told me I could have my own gang."

"Isn't that good?"

"Doesn't mean we'll be on our own. Means we'll be tossed the hot potatoes the main family doesn't want to deal with. He'll suck up our profits until we've nothing left to eat with."

"You mean we won't be making money?"

"Gotta figure out how."

The man was pinching at the new tablecloth, but not as hard as before; it didn't wrinkle as much.

"The Boss hasn't got much longer. That's what's got him thinking. By making me head a gang of my own, I won't be the one to take over."

"Right, we'll have to branch off from the main family."

"That war made me sure I was next in line. Dammit, that's what everybody was saying. I guess it frightened the Boss."

The waiter wheeled in a selection of cakes.

"Pick," the man said.

"Can I pick two?"

"Two, three, whatever."

The young guy pointed. The waiter bowed, sliced the

cakes and placed them on plates. The man picked one as well.

"I wanted to refuse, but there was that phone call. He went ahead and made the decision for me and just left."

Using only his fork, the young guy shoved a whole slice of cake into his mouth.

"That's fucking gross. Don't eat like that. This is one of the best restaurants in Tokyo."

"I agree."

The coffee arrived. And two cognacs, the man insisted.

"Who'll be taking over if you aren't?"

"Boss must be considering Kurauchi. Who knows, he could change his mind again. If I'm getting my own gang, I outrank Kurauchi, for now. Need to gain ground while that's true."

The young man had just gobbled down his last slice. "I see, so whenever the main family sends us the summons to help out with their wars, we gotta minimize our casualties. It'd be stupid losing our guys like that. And in the meantime we'll expand our business."

Smoke was rising from the man's cigarette in the ashtray. He casually poured out his coffee in it. There was a sizzling sound.

"Counting you, I got eight. Only eight. I'm gonna put you in charge of the younger guys."

"If something happens to the Boss, Brothers Kurauchi and Sano will go at each other for sure. It'll split the main family."

"I know branching out isn't bad if we play it right. I've never really busted my ass, in case something like this should come up. Good thing I'm not totally burned out ."

The man started picking at the tablecloth again. The cigarette butt was floating in the coffee-filled ashtray. He stared at it and then called for another ashtray.

"Right away, sir." The waiter went over to the small stand in the corner of the room and got out an ashtray. He left the room, carrying the one filled with coffee.

"You'll have to trade in your car for a Mercedes."

"Nah, the one I got now'll do. I'll get a Mercedes when I'm really boss. Got some business to take care of first."

"I'll be your driver. Can't leave that to any of the young ones."

"Hey, you gotta teach them. How to steer in combat, all the tricks. I need you for bigger stuff than driving."

"I understand."

"How much time have you done?"

"One year, only."

"Be prepared to do more."

"I already am. Just gotta make sure any I do is for the gang and not for being a fucked-up individual."

"You'll be surprised how good a strategist I am. It isn't like the old days. It takes more than guts now." He threw his napkin down on the table and walked out.

The young guy stared at the coffee in front of him for a while. The waiter brought in the brandy glasses. The young guy ran his finger along the edge of the rim. It made a clear sound.

"Bro's right, he's pretty smart," he muttered to himself. "Can't be bad for me either. Already I'm junior boss."

He ran his finger over the rim of the glass again. He repeated the motion over and over, entranced by the sound it made.

The man came back. The young guy stopped only for a moment before he started up again.

"This makes such a cool sound."

"Fuck your cool sound." The man got out a cigarette.

The young guy offered him a light.

"Finish that up and bring the car around."

"Okay." The young guy brought the glass to his lips and tilted it slowly. He kept it tilted even when it was empty. "I'll bet this wasn't cheap."

"Who cares? It's on the Boss."

The young man got up with a bow and left the room.

"A boss mustn't seem too rich." The man was talking to himself again. He pinched at the tablecloth. He started jiggling his knee. His heel tapped on the carpeting, but it made no sound.

Smoke was rising from the cigarettes in the ashtray again. He stared at it for a while.

"Sir, the car," the waiter announced.

"Yeah, I'm coming." He didn't let go of the tablecloth. "Fucking gourmet bastard," he muttered. Then silence. He looked up at the ceiling. The floor. The wall. He was still pinching at the tablecloth. "You'll see how much I learned in this damn business." Spit was flying from his mouth. It fell on the new tablecloth.

"Since I was nineteen." He shook his head several times. "Eight years behind bars." He finally let go of the tablecloth.

He started to get up, but sat back down. He smoothed out the tablecloth, and then stopped. It was wrinkled and stood up a bit where he had been pulling on it.

He took a closer look.

He could hear the sound of plates clanking outside the room. They must have been clearing off some of the tables. Standing up, he pinched the tablecloth again at the wrinkled spot and carefully pulled it higher and higher up.

He threw a parting glance at the pyramidal bulge as he walked out of the room.

# A S H E S

A single-flower vase sat on the table.

One of the walls was made of glass, providing a clear view of the cars driving up to the hotel entrance.

The man suddenly grabbed the sleeve of a waiter walking by and gestured towards his ashtray. The waiter, not understanding, stared back and forth between his sleeve and the man's face.

"What's wrong with you? Can't you see there're two cigarette butts sitting there?"

Blushing slightly, the waiter bowed deeply. He changed it for a new one. The man stared at it carefully, and put down the cigarette he had been smoking. His cigarette went out with a sizzle, its tip sucking a drop of water.

"Look at that. You brought me a wet ashtray."

The waiter became flustered, and blushed a shade deeper.

"And I was still smoking that one."

"I'm terribly sorry, sir." The waiter made as to reach for the ashtray, just to pull back his hand each time.

"What are you gonna do about it?" the man asked, his voice low. The waiter had a tortured look on his reddened face. A young man came over to the table and sat down across the man, looked up at the waiter, and grinned.

A man who looked like the manager, dressed in black, rushed over with an unopened pack of cigarettes and offered it to the man, bowing deeply. The waiter bowed low, too, like some kind of puppet.

"It's all right. Never mind." The man accepted the pack and tore it open casually. The manager led the waiter off.

"Boss, you're not a punk anymore. Would you please not act like one?"

"You think I did all that just for a smoke?"

"Was there some other reason?"

"Didn't like the way he looked at me." The man put a cigarette in his mouth. The younger man offered him a light, his thick gold bracelet tapping rhythmically against his lighter.

There weren't many people in the hotel tea lounge in the mornings. Only the two men seated by the window, and a young couple seated opposite one another, chatting away in the corner. The background music was some old Russian folk song that might have been in a school music book.

"So Kurauchi says he's going to come down?"

"Yeah. I looked in on him before, and there was some cute little number tucked away in his bed." The young man lifted up his little finger and grinned knowingly.

"So he's got the main family, and I'm supposed to be satisfied with starting a branch family. I don't fucking like it."

"You can't say that for sure, Boss. It's not definite yet, and you don't even know if Kurauchi Brother can bind them all under him at the main family—some of them don't trust him."

"So I just gotta keep still."

"That's the most sensible thing to do. I'm not sure about interfering as a relative and taking a pounding. Better off waiting until Brother messes up. Then let them come to you begging."

"They'll have plucked the hairs outta my ass by the time that happens." The man angrily ground out his cigarette. He had barely smoked it.

The hefty portable phone on the seat started ringing. The young man answered in a brusque manner, his bracelet jangling.

"It's from Munakata."

The man took the phone and stuck another cigarette between his lips. The young man offered him a light.

"What limit?" The man turned in his seat, facing his reflection in the wall of glass.

"You piece of shit, you haven't even stuck with it long enough, and you're fucking trying to talk smart. We gotta get by right now—one way or another. Do you hear me? Otherwise we'll be crushed. That's why you're out there collecting in the first place."

He was speaking in a suppressed growl. He could have been staring either at his reflection in the window or at the cars sliding to a stop at the entrance.

"Let 'em commit suicide, if they want. But don't let 'em until they've paid up. And don't come back until they do."

A bar of ash was about to fall from his cigarette. The young man got him an ashtray. He was too late, and the ashes fell on the table.

"The Boss over at the main family thinks I got all this cash already. No, he's not coming. Kurauchi is. He's gonna come and beg me for it. But that's just today. They don't mean to go on begging forever." He stopped talking. He threw the phone back at the young man.

"Got it? Three o'clock. The boss and I'll be back at the office by three." While the young man spoke, his boss kept poking at the ashes on the table.

Putting down the phone, the young man said, "He better shape up if our new branch isn't gonna be a bad mistake."

The waiter passing by their table stopped and quickly changed the ashtray and wiped the dark stain on the table. He wiped it first with a damp cloth and then a dry one.

The two men sat facing one another, smoking. Four customers walked in, passed by their table, and took a table all the way in the back. The young couple chatted on obliviously.

The young man stared at the four new customers. He looked bored. For a moment, their laughter drowned out the background music.

Ten minutes later, another man walked in and came over to their table. The young man scrambled to his feet and pulled out a chair. He bowed, and remained standing.

"So it's almost a month since we last met, Tanaka Brother."

"Something like that."

"Time flies. What, four months since you got your family together, and your branch is already our best."

"There're only four. And the other three are run by our Uncles, anyhow. I was the first one to get my own gang."

"Yeah, well, no surprise. Boss couldn't have come this far without you."

The waiter came to take their order. Coffee, the young man instructed, holding up three fingers.

"Why don't you sit," the man said. The young man bowed his head but made no move to sit down.

"So anyway, Kurauchi, you came for the monthly dues."

"The Boss's counting on the money."

"You're the junior boss of the main family. Can you get a postponement for me? Just five or six days." The man put a cigarette in his mouth. The young man held out a light. Kurauchi wrinkled up his face in disgust as the smoke blew in his direction.

"Someday you're gonna take over after the Boss. By then my branch'd be something to reckon with, and I'd back you up. It's up to you and me to see to it that the main family has grown by the time you inherit it. Because you know, Uncle and others prefer it to stay right where it is."

"Exactly, exactly, since they're the same generation as

the Boss. Best they can hope for is wardship. But Bro, I never really thought about it, you know."

"Hey, Kurauchi, there's no one else. I'll take care of things. I have enough power to back you up."

"Well, if your branch and the main family get on the same wavelength, that'll put an end to all the outside interference. And when I say that, I'm putting aside the question of who'll be Boss."

"Who else but you? There's no one."

Tanaka put out his stubby cigarette, grinding it into in the ashtray. The coffee arrived. Steam rose out of the cups.

"About the money. If it's just five more days, I can have that arranged. It's got nothing to do with me being set to take over. Between brothers like you and me, it isn't even a favor, it's only decent."

"Yeah, thanks."

"Boss's gotten short-tempered in his old age. Maybe that's what got him on your case, too, Brother."

"I owe you one. Let's think of it that way." The man put another cigarette between his lips, and the young man held out a light. Kurauchi made exaggerated attempts to wave the smoke away. The man continued blowing smoke out of his mouth, as though he had not even seen Kurauchi's gestures.

"Then we understand each other, Tanaka Brother? There's someplace I gotta be now—as the Boss's rep. I think we're finished here?"

He got up from the table. The young man bowed

deeply and led the way.

The three coffees on the table had turned cold.

"All I can do is blow smoke at him," the man muttered. He was not exhaling smoke at the moment, just staring down at the cigarette between his fingers. The background music had switched to a light, lively melody. The couple in the back got up and walked out.

"Yeah, with a cigarette," Tanaka muttered again.

The young man came back through the tea lounge and sat down across from Tanaka.

"So it looks like Brother's gonna go along with it. Guess it doesn't hurt to ask." He downed the cold cup of coffee in one gulp.

The man blew out smoke like he'd come to, and put out his cigarette.

Three young women came in and sat at the table next to them. "I'll bring in the dessert tray for you," the waiter told the women.

The man got up and walked out.

The young man glanced over at the women from time to time. They were engrossed in gossip, about a friend of theirs. When the waiter came back wheeling in a cake tray, their voices switched to a different pitch of delight.

About five minutes later, the man returned.

He gestured to the waiter to clear the table. The waiter placed the cold cups of coffee on his tray with great care, and held one in his hand. The manager came over and gave them a new ashtray.

"I can't get over how patient you were, Boss. When you ask, even Brother Kurauchi can't refuse."

"I went and looked in the mirror."

"You mean in the bathroom?"

"I looked like a guy who's always going to be taking orders. That's what I looked like."

"No way."

"Yeah, if I go on like that with Kurauchi, I'll be kissing his ass one day. That's what it's like between men."

"It's not like things have been decided already. We got ten young guys in our gang, you know."

"It'll be fifteen, then twenty. Then fifty, then seventy, then a hundred."

"The main family isn't so big that we can't catch up, you know."

"I have a good junior boss."

"I try to see what you don't, Boss. I worry about things you don't. That's my duty. But it hasn't been hard. I'm the kind of guy who thinks things have a way of turning out all right."

"Yeah well, I can be neurotic, so maybe you're all right that way."

The women had finished their cakes and were back to gossiping. The waiter came by from time to time to see if the ashtray had been used.

The man got a cigarette out, slowly, deliberately, and put it between his lips. The young man offered him a light.

"I can't go around taking orders from people like some

flunky. I can't let him call the shots when I used to outrank him. Kurauchi made me feel that way just now."

"You're not a flunky. The Boss wants Brother Kurauchi to be the next boss, so he asked you to get your own gang together. I think you're right about that. But this could be your chance, depending on how you see it."

"Could be." The man blew out cigarette smoke. He didn't look like he cared.

It wasn't quite lunch time, and no one was coming in the tea lounge to eat yet.

The phone rang.

"That so? Yeah, got it." The young man didn't hand over the phone this time. He fingered his bracelet as he spoke. "Sure, I'm free." He hung up and gave Tanaka a wry smile. "That was Mutoh. That construction project we talked about, he says things look pretty good. I'll go and give it another push."

"Yeah, if we got that going, it'll ease things."

The young man nodded again. The man put out his cigarette and glanced over at the hotel entrance.

"I'll be heading out. Got to take care of a few things," the young man said. The man nodded.

Alone now, he got out a cigarette and lit it himself. The women had their heads together, gossiping, but he showed no interest in them.

He dropped the ashes on the table rather than in the ashtray. The waiter saw this and came over to wipe the table.

"Don't touch it. Just leave it, will you?"

The waiter blushed. He bowed slightly and drew back.

The second time he flicked his cigarette, he dropped the bar of ashes so it was lined up next to the first cylinder. He dropped a third and a fourth, and after the fifth, put out the cigarette. The ashtray contained the butt and nothing else.

"Can't let an underling get ahead," he muttered.

Then he muttered the same words a second time. The women were laughing. Two men came in and sat at the table where the couple had been sitting. The waiter took their order and told the kitchen, two coffees.

"Crushed," the man muttered. With his finger, he crushed the leftmost bar of ash. Still muttering things, he crushed the other bars of ash slowly and deliberately. Five dark stains appeared on the table.

He wiped his finger on the back of the chair.

"It's easy to crush 'em."

The voices of the men mingled with the women's laughter. No one paid any attention to the background music.

"If they don't crush me, I'll crush them. Like ashes," the man muttered, staring at the five stains on the table.

Six more people came in, and the tea lounge was suddenly full of life. The man didn't look at any of them.

He lit another cigarette. He started dropping the ashes directly over the stains. The waiter only glanced at the stains each time he passed the table.

In a short while, the five stains had grown in size.

"Wait and see who's gonna be the lackey." Getting up, he took his wallet out of the inner pocket in his jacket and headed toward the cash register.

The waiter avoided heading over to the stained table for a good while. Two more people walked in. There was now a din in the tea lounge.

"Lowlifes," muttered the waiter, as he swept off the table with a damp cloth. The stains were still there, and he started scrubbing at them.

"You pay for those cigarettes, understand?" It was the manager. His hair, brushed back from his forehead, was jet black, but there were wrinkles around his eyes.

"Me?"

"That's right. I've told you before not to put out damp ashtrays."

"There was only one drop in there! He purposely put his cigarette in it. He wanted to make trouble right from the start."

"Even so, you have to pay for them. You got off easy. Better be grateful."

"You think they were *yakuza*?"

"Who knows. None of our business."

"Still! Pisses me off. I don't even smoke."

"Tough."

"Is it coming? Are you gonna tell me 'that's life'?"

"A pack of cigarettes was all it took. That's life too."

"I guess so. When he grabbed me, I thought I was in for

it."

"If he had smashed up the place, that would have been a big loss. Anyway, make sure you put that money for the pack in the cash register."

The manager walked away. The waiter began wiping down the table again, vigorously. The table shook.

"Get all kinds around here." His face was as red as when the man had grabbed at him.

"Excuse me. Can we get some water over here?" A woman called from one of the tables.

"No, is that really truly true?" their gossip resumed.

"Well, I don't see why not."

The waiter brought over the water pitcher and filled up their glasses. The glasses immediately turned frosty.

He also poured out a little of the water onto the table he had been cleaning. He scrubbed it with his cloth. "It's not going to come out, is it," he muttered, looking over at a clean, spotless table.

The women burst into laughter. "It won't come out," the waiter repeated simultaneously.

The table shook as he wiped away.

Part Two

# Within the Man

# PRISON OF WATER

## 1

The bubbles stopped.

The tiny spout in the miniature rock was clogged. But the water was clear; it filtered through a layer of gravel on the bottom before it went up through the pump. Enough oxygen, too.

The goldfish liked bubbles. At least, it seemed to. If you sat looking at the tank long enough, you saw the fellow frolic among them. There were two spouts where air could come out of the pump. Thinking one was enough, I'd stopped up the other with a toothpick wrapped in paper. I bought the rock with the plastic tube in it one day when I'd decided bubbles would be nice.

Almost a year since I bought a goldfish. One of those large ones with long tails. Somehow I thought one would do. Its tail was much longer now than when I had bought it.

"The bubbles are your only friends," I muttered to myself.

I picked up the habit around three or four years ago. Working for that greedy old man, it was the only way to stay sane. I could curse him all I wanted in cars, in bathrooms, in places where he couldn't hear me.

But it didn't do me any good. I began to feel more and more pathetic, until finally I was cursing at myself. That's why I went into town often. I beat up civilians and did things myself that I should have left to the young ones.

It'd been like that for a few years. I thought I'd take over eventually, so I managed to put up with the Boss's demands. But then he told me to go set up a branch of my own. So I became a boss and was treated like a boss, but I also had to handle all of the risky business that the main family didn't want. It preferred getting a cut of the profits, and the demands just kept growing.

Then the Boss collapsed. The rival clan saw the opportunity and was poised to launch attacks. The Boss couldn't lead in his condition. He wouldn't have been able to anyway, so woefully past his prime he was.

If only I were there. That thought kept coming back, for a few days now. If I hadn't started a branch family, I'd be the one at the head of the troops. No one else wanted to lead our Clan in times of war.

But I was the boss of a branch family. We'd only have to send help if asked. And I could find excuses for not going myself.

Perhaps I was forced to branch out at a good time. My luck hadn't run out yet. In the last war we had dominated them, seventy-thirty. Thanks to me. This time, they meant business, and it wouldn't be so easy.

The goldfish did a flip in the tank. It only started doing that a month ago. It wasn't really what you'd call swimming. Maybe there was something wrong with it, but I chose to believe that the fellow was just yearning to get out of the tank.

I took the rock out of the tank. Its jagged surface was slimy. I scrubbed it clean with the kitchen scouring brush. I put it back and the bubbles came gurgling out.

"Your only friends are back." Talking to myself again. I had to kick the habit. Talking to yourself, that's senile stuff.

The phone rang. It was Sugimoto from the office.

"They're panicking over at Clan headquarters. Sano-san keeps screwing with whatever Kurauchi-san does. Nothing like that went on when Boss was there."

For just a second, when he said "Boss," I thought he meant the old man, but I was the only one Sugimoto called by that name. The boss of the main family he referred to as "the Clan Boss." And when he talked about Kurauchi or Sano, he no longer used the honorific "Brother."

"They want you, but I told them no in so many ways. No point in putting your life on the line for them."

"You're smarter than I thought."

Sugimoto was one of the junior members I took with me when I started my branch family. There were five other guys who followed me from the main family, and a pair joined us from the outside; I had eight "children" when I opened up shop. We now numbered twelve.

"In any case, let's keep the dope situation messy for now, so they'll believe us when we say our hands are full. The main family forced all the dangerous deals on us. Might as well take advantage of it at a time like this," Sugimoto said, and chuckled gleefully. Shouldn't take any risks. That much was true. At the same time, Sugimoto was a gambler, betting on me.

"I'm going to stay here a little longer," I said. "Maybe in a couple of days, I'll head over to the main family. Say my hellos."

I hung up.

The bubbles were streaming out. The fish did another strange flip in the water. I took out a cigarette and opened the door to the balcony.

It was a clear day. The glittering rays from the sun reflected off the windows on the complex opposite mine.

I moved to this apartment twelve years ago. Even back then, it was pretty run-down. Yet, when the ten or so buildings, grouped like a herd of tired old elephants, all had lights in their windows after dusk, they shed their tired skins and looked new.

That's why my favorite moment was when all the lights turned on. It'd probably be another hour.

"Fucking geriatric can't act big anymore. Can't even eat what he wants at the hospital. Just sleeping with a tube up his nose."

My words drifted out the window, along with the

cigarette smoke. I couldn't feel sorry for the old man, though he was stuck in a hospital, barely able to speak. He had been the kind of boss who only ever thought of bleeding his children dry.

I ground out my cigarette stub in the ashtray. It was full of cigarette butts. I got up, taking the ashtray with me, and tossed the butts in the trash.

It was a two-bedroom apartment with a dining room and kitchen. I kept things clean. No one would ever guess a *yakuza* lived here. I had my own family, but I never brought any of my men around here. We usually met at Ayumi's bar, or at her apartment. The bar and the apartment were both impressive, and it was mainly to make the kids happy that I had everyone meet there.

The phone rang again. It was the same phone I got a dozen years ago, when there was no such thing as adjusting the ringer volume. I threw a blanket over it when I wanted quiet.

I had a gut feeling about this one. Probably someone from the Clan. Sugimoto couldn't rightly keep my whereabouts a secret if Kurauchi or Sano really pressed him.

I let it ring and put on my jacket.

## 2

It looked like they had just opened.

I glanced over at the four girls sitting on the sofa and went over to the counter and sat down.

Ayumi came out from the back. "Sano-san from the main family called for you. He said to call him back right away." She wore kimonos more often now that she had this place. The other place had just been her and the bartender.

The one who benefited the most from my branching out was Ayumi. She took out loans, moved to a bigger location, and even bought a big apartment in Shibuya. I'd been with her for nine years, and I chose Ayumi to be the Big Sis for my "children." We weren't married, and legally her place couldn't be traced to me. But the income from the place was mine; I was the real owner. Ayumi would never use the paperwork to try to steal the place from me. She knew all too well that she'd be killed, or that I'd make her whore to pay me for it.

"He'll probably call again. Tell him I'm not here."

"Sugi-chan already told me to say that, but Sano-san might actually come here, you know."

"If he does, he does. They're just trying to figure out how to put me to use."

Ayumi stopped asking me to quit being a *yakuza* after I started my own family. And she'd been the one who always used to tell me, "Now's the time to quit." I didn't mope to anyone about the simplicity of women. What'd be the point of that?

"Bartender, bourbon soda."

The bartender, Fujii, was the actual father of one of my "kid brothers" who was in jail. Fujii had thirty years of bartending experience. "God, he's covered in moss," Ayumi said, when he first came to work for her. Somewhat out of character for me, I responded that that was what gave his cocktails flavor.

Fujii's son killed a man for a stupid reason. Saying the reason was just stupid, the Boss refused to look after his parents. It was a matter of honor for the Clan, but that didn't seem to sway the Boss. His stance was that if a clan had to take care of people every time someone got pissed off and committed murder, it'd go bankrupt.

But it was people who killed in a fit of rage that ended up as *yakuza*. That was my take on it. What did the Boss expect from people who had to join our world?

Fujii silently placed my bourbon soda on the counter. He hadn't stirred it. He knew how I liked it.

Two more years before his boy got out. It had been a *yakuza* fight, in which he'd gotten badly hurt himself, but he was sentenced to four years and six months anyway. The law ought to stop giving a damn about *yakuza* fights and just let us kill each other in peace.

"Do you want to call Sugi-chan?"

"I got a portable phone, you know."

"Why don't you get yourself a Mercedes with one of those telephone antennas?"

"Don't be stupid. I'm not like the Clan Boss."

"You'll want one someday. You'll definitely want one."

"You're the one who wants one."

I tossed back my bourbon soda. There were six girls employed at the place. None were absent. An Akasaka club with six girls working it. If things got going, this place would make good money.

Making women work for you. Most *yakuza*, if they had any brains, did it. But the Boss wouldn't even do that much. Instead, he made me branch off so he could milk me.

"Anyway, you can't get in touch with me. Remember that."

Fujii made me another bourbon soda. A younger brother had killed a man. Wasn't it a *yakuza*'s duty to look after the kid's parents while the kid was doing time? Even if it wasn't for the good of the clan. It could easily have been me.

I was nineteen. The Boss was young back then, full of real swagger. I was just a cheap punk, too scared to say two words to him. That was more than twenty years ago. And eight of those years I spent on the inside. Going to prison, I told myself it was for the good of the Clan, for the good of the Boss. But only the first two times. The other two times I was cuffed, I just felt resigned. The life—serving terms was part of it.

"I doubt they'd strike all the way over here."

Even though it was the main family that was locking horns, there was no being sure the enemy wouldn't come after the branch families. Still, it was hard to imagine that they'd come after this club. If I were them, I'd leave this kind of place alone.

Fujii spoke without looking up from polishing a glass. "Though I'm not sure I'd be of any use—"

"If you get hurt or arrested, I won't be able to face the Fujii who's already inside."

"So is it better if we called the cops?"

"This is a civilian establishment, and that's how it's listed in the books."

"Yes, I understand, but…"

I'd told him to go ahead and call the cops in case of trouble. If he did, the troublemakers would have their hands tied. I knew they didn't really want that.

"A gang needs a clean place like this, where people like you can work."

"Yes, Sister has told me."

"Let's get one thing straight. You're not one of mine. When you talk about Ayumi, call her Mama-san like they usually do in clubs. Only my kids need to call her Big Sister."

I lit my cigarette with my Dupont. When I started the branch family, the Boss gave me his old lighter. I wasn't some kid who could be bought off with a second-hand lighter. I just figured it'd put the main family at ease if they saw me using it all the time.

Customers came in. The girls welcomed them. Some of my guys' wives and future wives could join the troupe someday. A married guy going off to jail had reason to worry. If his wife worked here, then a year or two wouldn't seem like such a big deal.

I finished my second bourbon and went outside, a cigarette in my mouth.

I got in the car and called the Clan headquarters on my portable phone.

"It's Tanaka. Someone there?"

"Yes, Brother Kurauchi is." The young guy at the phone sounded nervous. Kurauchi came to the phone right away.

"What's going on, Tanaka Brother?"

"You mean why aren't we being more supportive?"

"We're not asking you to be 'supportive', for God's sake. The Clan's at war, and that means you are too."

"What'd the Boss say?"

"You know he can't really talk. And that's why you haven't even sent us your junior members."

"Now wait a minute, Kurauchi-san." I glanced at my watch and checked the level of gasoline in the tank. "You accusing me of shirking my duties just because the Boss is sick?"

"Sure looks like it."

"Would you mind saying that again, Kurauchi-san?"

Kurauchi didn't say anything. He was a smart guy. He must have known immediately that it was bad news to make an enemy of me now. Kurauchi and his calculations. Sano, the most senior of the senior officers, was always easily outmaneuvered by him. I had been outmaneuvered too. This time, though, it was my turn to screw him over.

In times of war, it didn't help you out much to be smart in Kurauchi's way.

"You don't have to take it that far, Brother."

"Don't try to appease me. Don't you know what the Boss told me? When he could still talk. He said, 'Tanaka, I'm putting you in charge of drugs. Protect the business *at all costs.*' If you're really telling me to go against those direct orders from the Boss, then I'm coming right away. But let me tell you, we don't have it easy. They're all trying to filch our routes, seeing that the main family is stumbling."

"The drug routes are important, of course."

"Whose fault is it that the main family is stumbling, Kurauchi-san?"

"Would you please drop the 'san', Brother?"

"You're the whole Clan's junior boss. I can't simply call you 'Kurauchi', can I?"

"In any case, things aren't looking good."

"And whose fault is it?"

"No one's. It's because the Boss is ill."

"I see. So the Boss can't even go getting sick now."

"That's not what I meant," Kurauchi said imposingly. "They're trying to take advantage of the Boss's illness. We need to stick together in a pinch like this. That's what I meant."

"That's pretty fucking obvious."

"So what's the problem?"

"Kurauchi-san, what am I supposed to do? Do I protect

the drug routes that the Boss told me to guard with my life, or do I throw them away? That's what I'm asking. I can only be in one place at a time. When things are all screwed up like this, I don't know which way I'm supposed to go. If you tell me it's okay to let the dope go, then I'll happily do it right away. The cops are getting suspicious, anyhow."

"I'm not saying you should do that."

"That's what it sounds like to me. There's no way I can handle both right now. You have to decide which one it's going to be, Kurauchi-san."

"Let's be honest with each other, Brother. This isn't getting anywhere."

"Honesty is exactly what I've been giving you. I don't know what to do. I'm asking for your advice."

"So you have no intention of helping out the Clan."

"Weren't you listening to me, Kurauchi-san? What the fuck, if that's what you think, I'm coming over right away."

"So you'll help out after all?"

"Yeah. Except, I won't be able to keep my word to the Boss. So let's do this. I'll forget his orders, but you put it in writing that you, as acting boss, told me to forget his orders."

"You're getting nasty, Tanaka Brother."

"And you? You insinuated that I was being disloyal."

"So in other words, you don't want to give us a hand."

"Enough is enough, Kurauchi-san! Better not provoke me, the drug situation's made me irritable. This isn't our first war with them. I had them just where we wanted them. It was my responsibility to see to it back then. But now you're the one who's in that position, Kurauchi-san."

"And that's why I'm sending you the summons."

"What are the Uncles up to?"

"What about them?"

"Ah, so anything that's a little dangerous is our responsibility, huh? I get it. If that's why our gang was created, we're disbanding, today."

"Did I ask for your men to do all the fighting? I'm just asking you to report to headquarters."

"Kurauchi-san, I know I owe you. You negotiated the deadline for our monthly dues once, I haven't forgotten. That's why I've tried my best to be patient during this conversation. Anyway, I'll call my gang together and come over to help you. But you won't be negotiating deadlines for me again. 'Cause we won't be able to pay our monthly dues, period."

"What's nasty about you is the way you argue."

"In any case, call an officers' meeting. I'll say the same thing at that meeting."

"I'm asking you now, man to man."

"That's strange, Kurauchi-san. Is it a done deal? Are you taking over the Clan? Is that why you're ordering me around?"

"That's enough."

"So what about the meeting?"

"I said enough."

"Wait, Kurauchi-san. Don't tell me you were trying to

issue orders without the others' knowledge."

"Brother Tanaka, the Clan is facing a life or death situation at the moment."

"There ought to be a meeting then!"

"I'll call a meeting in due time."

"In due time?"

"Enough. Why do I have to beg you, anyway?" Kurauchi was pretty pissed off. Under his command, the officers at the main family were all facing in different directions. At this rate, there was no way he would become the successor.

"Being a *yakuza* is about sticking to principles. Can't believe I'm having to tell you that, Kurauchi-san."

"So if the officers agree, you'll send me as many troops as I need?"

"In fact, that's the decision I want, as soon as possible. I'm sick and tired of drug operations. I never asked to be responsible for the routes. Like I said, I owe you one. Arrange things for me just once more so I can pay you back sooner rather than later."

Kurauchi hung up.

I smoked a cigarette before turning on the engine.

Things were going according to plan so far. If I could sink Kurauchi and kept Sano under my thumb, I'd be able to start talking a different way. It would just take time.

I was about to pull out but reached for the phone once more.

"Let's meet at our usual place."

It was the only information I gave Sugimoto. During wartime, I took care not to give specific information over portable phones and car phones. I had to consider myself tapped. I bet that kind of thing didn't even occur to Kurauchi. It had to be the first time he was heading war efforts.

I lit a cigarette and drove off.

## 3

Yoshie's apartment was near the river in Nakameguro.

She was my mistress. Not that she was beautiful or had a great body. She was over thirty-five. There was one thing about her, though. She took immense pleasure in making other women miserable.

She had four girls working for her. All of them amateurs. A housewife, two career girls, and an art school student. Yoshie found them on her own, and also brought them customers. In other words, prostitution. My job was to protect her from interference by other gangs.

Yoshie had a one-bedroom apartment. She didn't live extravagantly. She lived quietly. My cut was only thirty percent of what she made, so she must have had extra dough, but she didn't seem to be too interested in spending it.

That made for a valuable kind of woman. To let her

know that I wasn't using her, I slept with her. Since then, she took good care of me, and when I had to use her place, she disappeared discreetly for about half an hour or so.

I thought one day I'd start sending girls to work for her. Put ten women to work, and you can end up making good money.

I had already contacted Yoshie, so the door was unlocked when I got there.

"You didn't come to make love, did you?"

"Why, you want to?"

"Once a month would be nice."

"Later. Sugimoto's coming by."

"Oh."

Yoshie started telling me about a fifth girl she had her eye on. She worked the cash register at a supermarket.

"If you need dope to keep her around, I can get you some at cost."

"I'll take you up on that sometime. That's for when I find a girl I'd enjoy seeing crawl in hell."

"Too bad you're a woman. You would've made a good *yakuza*."

"Are you a good *yakuza*?"

"No, I'm no good. I tend to quit somewhere along the way. Right now I'm trying to move up in the world, so I'm trying not to quit on it. But usually I stop giving a damn and quit."

"I think I know why you became a *yakuza*, now that we've spent all this time together."

"Tell me why?"

"Oh, I have a hunch."

The doorbell rang.

Sugimoto came in and Yoshie set two beers on the dining room table. She left the apartment wearing a pair of sunglasses. It seemed her four girls already had regular customers.

"I think we ought to give it another twist," I said, pouring Sugimoto a beer. Sugimoto looked at me questioningly. I poured until the foam started to spill over, and Sugimoto quickly took a sip.

"Pretend you're Kurauchi."

"Well, I think I'd suspect that the drug troubles stuff was an excuse."

"It'd be different if there really were some kind of trouble."

"Well, I'll see what I can do."

"If it were me, I wouldn't be fooled too easily."

Sugimoto gulped down his beer. I lit a cigarette. Sugimoto forgot to offer me a light, he was so preoccupied. If things didn't work out for me, Sugimoto would lose his chance at moving up, too. That sort of relationship between men was a good thing.

"Is there someone we can send to jail for a while?"

"You want me to go, is that it?"

"No. Until our branch is solid, I can't afford that. There's no need to send you inside."

"How about Mutoh? He's already twenty-two."

Sugimoto poured a beer for me. I took a swig. "Can you persuade him?"

"How many years will it be?"

"Four, maybe."

"That should be fine. He's got it in him to make it through. But boss, if we hit them, we'd be on the front lines. We'd have more of a voice in the Clan, but aren't we too small to be hitting that gang?"

"Don't make me laugh. I told you I wanted a *twist*."

My cigarette had burned down. I lit another one. By the time Sugimoto had scrambled around and found a light, I was already flipping the lid of my Dupont shut.

"Remember that guy Kajita?"

"The kid who used to hang around Yoshimoto."

"He's not legal yet, is he."

Yoshimoto was one of the juniors at the main family. During the last war, he'd tried to go over to the enemy with his lackey Kajita. I managed to trap Yoshimoto into knocking off one of the higher-ups on the enemy side instead. Thanks to me, he didn't have to become a traitor.

Knocked off the enemy officer, and truce talks followed. We came out of that war seventy-thirty.

"Can we use Kajita as a hit man?"

"Wait a minute, Boss. He's practically on the enemy side. Even if they still don't trust him, because of Yoshimoto."

"That's why he's perfect."

"I don't understand. What do you mean?"

I looked at Sugimoto's face and grinned. The *yakuza* life was all about how much pain you could take. That's what the Clan Boss taught me. Sounded good, but in all the twenty years I'd been with him, I never once saw him take any pain.

"He's a hit man for the enemy."

Had Kajita actually offered to be a hit man for the enemy, to regain their trust, it would certainly make a lot of sense. In fact, if he wanted to continue being a *yakuza*, that was his only option.

"The enemy? Meaning he's going to target Kurauchi-san or Sano-san?"

"Kurauchi and Sano—and Kawano—have been my rivals, but we've eaten out of the same rice bowl. So have you, Sugimoto. I'm not so bent on moving up that I'd go around knocking off old pals." But I didn't mean it. There were any number of times when I wished someone would rub out the Boss—and thoroughly meant it. There were even times when I wanted to strangle him with my bare hands. Indeed, one day, Sugimoto could start feeling that way about me.

"Got it, Sugimoto? Kajita's gonna try to bump me off. I told you I wanted a twist. There's the little twist."

"So of course, you don't intend to let Kajita actually knock you off."

"No, but I wouldn't mind another scar. We'll have to kill Kajita afterwards, though. Somewhere lonesome."

"I think I'm beginning to understand."

Sugimoto poured himself another beer. I ground out my cigarette. I was on to something brilliant.

"In other words, you get targeted by the enemy, Boss, and we rub out Kajita."

"And I'll tell the whole Clan beforehand that we'll be fighting on the front lines. I get hurt, and they'll all think we're the only ones who're out there fighting. We'll be in a position to tell Kurauchi and Sano to hurry up and pitch in."

"Of course."

"The question is whether Mutoh can handle Kajita."

"I'll do it." Sugimoto put his glass on the table. He had hardly touched it. "I'll take care of it. That way, we can be sure."

"We can't risk having you locked up."

"Then we'll have Mutoh do it."

"Can you handle all the arrangements?"

"Trust me. I'll have everything ready by tomorrow night."

"Use a knife on Kajita, got it?"

"I understand."

"Well, I'd better go to the Clan headquarters now."

"Please take Munakata with you. And another junior member. A boss shouldn't appear all alone."

"Yeah, okay." I lit up another cigarette and Sugimoto downed his beer.

"You've got to stop going around like one of the young ones, you know. I'm only saying it because…well, sometimes you don't act like you're supposed to. It worries me, you know."

"Sometimes I wonder why I've stayed in this world for so long. More than twenty years. There's a part of me that resists being a real *yakuza*. I just don't fit. That's probably why the Clan Boss started to dislike me."

"I was saying, you're not a punk anymore."

"Yeah, I know that." Why did I become a *yakuza*? Maybe I'd had no choice.

"When are you going to headquarters?"

"A little later'll be better. I'll try and look like I barely kept the drug war under control for the day. Like I really shouldn't be there."

"I'll put in a call, tell them it looks like you can get over there. I'll tell them to wait for you." Sugimoto laughed out loud. I got up and got another beer from the fridge.

"One thing. All this is strictly between you and me. Don't tell Mutoh either what we're really up to."

"I understand." Sugimoto yanked the tab off his second can of beer.

I knew I would be all right. I was sure I'd have no problem dodging some kid's sloppy attempt with a knife. Still, it was a dangerous plan. The fact that there was some true danger pleased me.

Suddenly, I felt something like sexual desire.

I kept looking over at the door, sipping at my beer and wishing Yoshie would hurry up and come back.

4

I got out of the car at Shinjuku.

I waved off Munakata, who started to come with me, and walked off alone. It was already 11:30, but there were still plenty of people out on the street.

I had arrived at Clan headquarters at 10:30.

Kurauchi, Sano, and Kawano were all seated and waiting. I let them know I'd take charge of the war operations, but I'd do what I could to keep the drug operations. Consequently, I couldn't send any of my men to defend the headquarters. But as soon as the fighting started, we'd come right away, in three cars. We'd bring our own guns too.

No one opposed my plan.

Three officers nodded in agreement when I said there was no point in having my men sitting around at headquarters waiting for things to flare up. Two younger officers, who'd just been promoted, remained standing the whole time I spoke.

I would supply eleven men. The main family could round up forty. My eleven would serve as the assault unit to take it to the enemy headquarters if and when our own came under attack. Since I wasn't serious, I managed to make the most exorbitant promises with utmost cool. Munakata, who had tagged along, was in shock.

My speech lasted fifteen minutes. Very few interruptions. I even succeeded in giving them the impression that it wouldn't be at all preposterous for our branch to retain as much as half of the drug profits every month, for our pains.

I took a swig of the scotch put out in front of me, staring at Kurauchi, who was looking at me like he'd done me in. When really I was the one who'd done him in.

Shinjuku was pretty far from the main family's territory, and it was far from mine, too. There weren't any other organizations nearby either. I did my best to avoid any shady-looking areas and kept on walking. I found myself in a big crowd without really meaning to.

I came across an arcade. I spent about fifteen minutes inside, and then ducked into a small bar, drank two glasses of whiskey.

I didn't really know what I was doing. Once upon a time, I used to walk around like this—without any real purpose—in the entertainment district. I couldn't stand being cooped up in a room for more than two days. By the third day, I always had to get out. I've been like that since high school.

My old man was a carpenter and an alcoholic. I was in and out of a lot of bars because I had to carry him home when he got too drunk to walk straight. I was intrigued by the excitement of the city because I thought there had to be *something* happening in that downtown hubbub.

My old lady shacked up with some guy in Kyushu, and I haven't seen her since I was twelve. I don't even know if she's dead or alive. I don't particularly want to talk to her, and I don't want to be reminded of her, either.

"So what company do you work for?" It was the girl next to me.

I'd moved on to my second bar. Gray suit, understated tie. It was a sort of uniform. It didn't even occur to me that I might look like a respectable businessman. A few months after I graduated from high school, I ran into one of my old classmates, and he was dressed in a suit. With his gray suit and understated tie, he looked every bit the adult.

I became an apprentice to a civil engineer at a construction company, but I quit over an argument with one of my co-workers. After that, I couldn't get anything you'd call real work. The longest job I held down was bartending. That lasted eight months.

It was around that time when I met the Boss.

"It's small. You wouldn't have heard of it," I answered.

"Oh, size doesn't matter, you know what I mean? In my case, anyway, I don't get asked to do after-hours entertaining. It's enough to put in an honest day's work."

I worked pretty hard myself. Mine wasn't a job where you could get away with slacking off. An honest day's work? I threatened honestly, I stabbed honestly.

"So how old are you?"

"Twenty-one."

She looked young and fresh, as she should at that age. Almost like a child. For a second, I wondered how she'd do at the club in Akasaka, but Ayumi was extremely jealous. She'd only be suspicious if I took this girl there. Yoshie wasn't the jealous type, but her girls were for whoring.

"What's your name?"

"Yoko."

"I'm Tanaka."

"That's a lie."

"Why?"

"Since I started working here, I've already met three guys called Tanaka, and none of them was telling the truth."

"Here, my name is Tanaka."

"Wow, you're serious."

I'd shown the inside of my jacket, where my name was sewn in. Yoko clapped her hands with delight. I felt my heart stir at her silly expression of delight, and was surprised at myself for feeling that way.

I used to own girls like her in five minutes once we were alone. I sold off many like her. I'd get them addicted and have them work for me. One ended up killing herself.

Women are all the same once you've had them.

"So what kind of work do you do, Tanaka-san?"

"What do you think I do?"

"Manager at an electrical company."

"Really."

"Totally wrong?"

"No, not bad."

"Really? I've got a pretty good sense about these things."

I found the "manager" bit really amusing.

"I'll be back."

"No, don't go yet!"

"I got to make an early start tomorrow."

Yoko walked me all the way out. She was young, so she had a pretty good body.

"Really, Tanaka-san? You'll really come again?"

"Yeah, maybe next week. I'm a little busy this week." I waved good bye. I couldn't believe I waved. I kept thinking, once you sleep with 'em they're all the same.

"I'm crazy." My old habit was back. "Getting all worked up about some little girl." I paused, muttering. I continued walking again. "I'll own her. Set her up with some rich bastard, let her put the squeeze on him. I'll shoot her up with dope and hand her over to Yoshie." Whenever I muttered to myself, I stopped walking.

Two young guys leaning up against a telephone pole were laughing at me.

"Something funny, you punks?"

"Mumbling to yourself, old timer?"

"Old timer?" I said, and they doubled over with laughter. I kicked one of them in the shins. He groaned. The other one didn't seem to know what hit him.

"Hold on, old timer." I was about to walk away when I felt a hand grab my leg.

"You said something, punk?"

"Shut up. Why the fuck did you do that?"

"It's my job." I laughed. The one I kicked seemed really pissed off, and was glaring at me red-faced.

"Hope you don't got no plans for tonight, pa."

"Pa?"

"More like grandpa, really."

"I've got the time, if that's what you mean."

"You've got some spirit in you, geezer."

He grabbed my wrist. I shook him off. "I'm coming. Don't bother."

"Over there. There's no one around. You coming?"

"You're the one who asked, don't forget."

"You're not scared of much, are you."

He started walking. I followed silently.

We ended up between two buildings. The alley grew wider some ways in, but no one came through. I made such mental notes when I walked around entertainment districts.

"You look pretty green, punk. How old are you?"

"Probably half your age, old man. It'd take two of me to add up to your age. That's why we each get a chance at you. Fifty-fifty."

"You fight dirty, don't you? That's something a *yakuza*'d say. And I mean a cheap *yakuza*."

His fist came flying at me. It grazed my cheek. I felt the heat.

I maneuvered to create some distance. One of them didn't look too excited. Not that he was a coward, more like he just couldn't be bothered.

The kid threw another punch. I sank an elbow in the neck of the guy on my right. Without missing a beat, I kicked the other one in the stomach. With the second hit, he crumbled, and with the third, he bent over double. I kicked him several more times. His groaning stopped, and he began to spasm. The other one finally came at me from behind. I bit his little finger. In the next instant, I yanked it back hard. A sharp sensation like a damp branch snapping in the palm of my hand told me I'd broken it.

He crouched over, gripping his hand. I kicked him, aiming for his chin. Make him look real pretty. That's what I felt like doing.

I went for the eyes and nose. He shrieked. I stuck my shoe in his mouth and pressed my weight down on him.

"Let us go," he begged. Before he could get his words out, I kicked his mouth. Hands would hurt. Better to kick when you can.

"Mercy! You'll kill us!"

I kicked his nose. I kicked at the crotch of the one still curled up on the ground, unmoving. He screamed. His screams continued and eventually turned into moaning.

"Pretending I've knocked you out, ha? Think you've fooled me, kid?" I kept kicking at the crotch of the one trying to crawl away, too.

I lit up.

I circled them slowly, kicking them from time to time.

A punk. That's what I was. I used to get into fights like this all the time when I was younger, and there was a part of me that still wanted it.

One of them stopped moving. He wasn't dead. After I

became a *yakuza*, I became interested in figuring out what sort of blows could kill a guy. Not necessarily so that I wouldn't kill him, but so I could.

I stepped on the face of the guy who wasn't moving, putting the weight of my whole body on him for a moment. He groaned.

"Don't try to outsmart me, you little punk."

"Mercy!"

"Depends. Give me what you got."

"What?"

I pressed down on him again. He scrambled for his pockets, grabbing his wallet.

Three ten-thousand yen bills, and two one-thousand yen bills. There was only a five-thousand yen bill in the other one's wallet.

"That ain't enough."

"But that's all we have. That's everything." I stepped on his mouth. Four, five times. I heard something crack beneath the heel of my shoe. He could pay up this way. It was how *yakuza* settled accounts, and these guys were dealing with a *yakuza*.

I kicked the other guy in the crotch several times too.

"Don't go crying to the cops. I'll kill you for sure."

They just kept groaning.

I went out on the main road and walked for a bit before I hailed a cab.

"Kitasuna. The apartment complex."

The driver didn't say anything as we drove off.

"I'll own her. Then I'll sell her off. She'll be worth a lot, a little gem. That's how we do it."

I saw Yoko's laughing face appear before me.

I laughed too. But it wasn't with her.

I got out of the cab and walked up to the fourth floor. Apparently, all the new apartment complexes were high-rises and they even had elevators. The rents were outrageously expensive.

I noticed a button dangling from my jacket as I opened the door.

As soon as I went inside, I got out a needle and thread, moved a dining room chair over to the lamp and sewed on the button.

"My luck hasn't run out yet."

I wasn't thinking about Yoko anymore. My mind was on tomorrow.

I had a bath and changed, and I felt like a new man. It was almost three in the morning.

The goldfish started swimming around. Probably because I had turned on the light. He only needed to be fed once a day. That's what the guy at the pet store told me, but I grabbed a pinch of fish food and sprinkled it in. As an apology for waking him up.

He did that funny flip in the water. The bubbles were spewing out vigorously again. It'd be at least another month before it stopped up.

I got out a beer from the fridge and poured myself a glass. I watched the fish while having a smoke. He looked like he was having a harder time swimming now that his tail had grown so long, compared to when I first brought him home.

"That's the way things are."

I didn't really mean anything by it. I just felt that things were that way.

Man, I was tired.

5

It was a white car.

It passed under the street lamp for a second, and that was all I could make out.

I stayed in my car, waiting with the engine running. Headlights approached. The car slowed. I signaled for him to pass.

The white car stopped. He turned off the engine. What an idiot. You never turn off the engine in situations like this. Guys who weren't careful always got killed.

He got out of the car. It was Kajita, and he was still a skinhead.

As of now, everything was running smoothly. I switched off the room lamp and opened the door.

I approached him. The light was coming from behind me. It wasn't until I was within three meters of the car that Kajita realized it was me.

He squealed with surprise.

"Hey, Kajita. It's been a while."

Kajita couldn't speak.

"You know Yoshimoto's behind bars. All because he was unlucky enough to get acquainted with you."

"Tanaka Brother."

"You don't got any right to call me that. Why'd you call me out? Better be good."

"Call you out?"

"I came here because you asked. I thought maybe you wanted to clear things up. I like the attitude, so I didn't bother packing heat."

"Clear things up? Me?"

"Yeah. Clear things up about Yoshimoto. You've followed me, haven't you?"

"That's ridiculous!"

"Ridiculous or not, I'm gonna kill you."

"Stop it. It's not funny. Sugimoto-san told me—"

I glared at him. Kajita couldn't speak. Things were tense. I could still scare a guy into silence. I stepped forward. Kajita drew back. I kept glaring at him. I wasn't going to let him go. I made that much very clear. I wouldn't let him get away.

"Come 'ere, punk. I'm alone."

Kajita's eyes gave off a faint spark. We glared at each other. Felt like I could. Take him on. I could still handle a little punk.

The knife. It glinted in the palm of my hand. Kajita

pulled out one from behind his back, too. Its wooden sheath falling on the road made a dry, hollow sound.

We glared at each other for a while.

Kajita's breathing grew labored. Mine was still calm. That's the way things went. It was still too early to leave the tough jobs to young guys. Give it another ten years.

Kajita let out a yell.

We went for one other. Just once. That was my plan. Something hot sliced through my side. And I could tell my knife was digging flesh.

I felt the blood. "Dammit!" I took a deep breath. I didn't bother chasing after Kajita. He screamed and ran from me.

That was it. The engine wouldn't start right away, and he was panicking. Finally it turned over, and he sped off.

There had to be a pretty deep gash in Kajita's thigh. Sugimoto would take care of the rest.

I returned to the car and cut my shirt with the scissors I had brought along, applying gauze to the wound and taping it up. It wasn't deep, but it was long and there was a lot of blood.

"Might have to sew it up."

I couldn't go to a doctor for stitches. I'd do it myself, with a needle and thread. I had to do it once before to close up a wound.

I grabbed my portable phone.

"It's Tanaka. Anyone there?"

Kurauchi came to the phone right away.

"Are Sano-san and Kawano-san there?"

"Yes."

"Kurauchi-san, they're totally serious, are you gonna be able to handle it?"

"Handle what, Tanaka Bro?"

"They sent over a hit man. Stabbed me in the stomach. Dodged just in time so didn't get to my guts. They took advantage of the drug trouble and sneaked him in. I got my people tailing him now. I got him pretty good, too, so they'll probably catch 'em."

"A hit man?"

"They aren't kidding around."

"Brother, why didn't you have a gun with you?"

"Kurauchi-san." I lowered my voice. "Stay there. I'm heading over there. I'm going to kill you."

"What is it, Brother? What did I say?"

"What the hell kind of game do you think I'm playing? Dope. I'm the drug department. We're surrounded by secret investigators, undercover detectives. Who the hell packs heat with that kind of crowd except amateurs? If they find anything more than a knife on me, they'll bust me fair and square. In drugs you gotta obey the law, you see. And you're asking me, Kurauchi-san, why I'm not carrying a gun?"

"Brother."

"Things are so crazy now that they've put more cops on the trail. Do you know any of that when you tell me to hand over the profits? Kurauchi-san, sit tight!"

"Just a minute, Tanaka Brother. I believe I owe you an apology. I owe you more than an apology."

"I was thinking to go somewhere to sew up my wound. Now my heart's bleeding too."

"Brother, let's settle the profits issue right now. I was in the wrong. From now on, it'll be half, like you said. I'll see to it that you get what you deserve."

"Tanaka, it's me. What happened?"

I sensed someone take away the receiver, and heard Sano's voice. Sano was fifty-one already and was proxy to the Boss. He didn't have a morsel of ambition while the Boss was still healthy. But now, with Kurauchi emerging as the next boss, Sano worried himself sick over losing his sinecure.

"A hit man got me. Ask Kurauchi-san about the details. I've been stabbed."

"What did Kurauchi do wrong?"

"Forget about it. He seems to get it finally. Anyway, prepare for war. We're going to take care of that hit man—it's a matter of honor." That's all I said before I hung up.

I got out the car and drove on to the highway, headed for Kitasuna.

My side was starting to ache. You don't have to take it that far, Sugimoto had said, but I told him that if I didn't take it far enough, Kurauchi wouldn't believe me. Truth be told, maybe I just wanted to be in a knife fight.

Kurauchi completely disgraced himself. It was more than I had hoped for.

"Nine-tenths done."

I didn't speed. I arrived in Kitasuna in about forty minutes.

I threw my jacket in a bag, and put on a different one, so it wouldn't matter who saw me.

I stripped down to the waist in the apartment and boiled a needle and thread in a pot, and dipped my fingertips in to sterilize them. I sewed up the wound, leaving about a centimeter between stitches. I managed to endure the feeling of needle and thread pushing into my flesh. After I did six stitches, I applied the gauze again and taped it all up.

Better lay off the booze for a while. Stick to cigarettes.

Watching the goldfish do his funny flips in the water, I smoked four in a row.

"You want out, you punk?" I said. "The only place you can survive is in there."

My side was still aching. I drank double the recommended dose of painkillers.

"If you want out, use your smarts to figure out how. Little punks are the only ones who try to get what they can't. You'll never get out by turning cartwheels."

I was full of a feeling that felt like irritation. "Kurauchi, acting like nothing's wrong."

The goldfish kept at his flipping antics.

"The Boss still not giving it up. He's finished anyhow. I've got Kurauchi by his collar." I kept mumbling, but my irritation didn't go away.

The phone rang.

"How's it going, Tanaka? How's the wound?"

"It's about ten centimeters along the side. I sewed it up."

"Kurauchi gave me the low-down. All he's good at is accounting, you know."

"Let it drop."

"Well, I'm getting things ready, anyway."

"They nearly got me. That decided things. It's all right. It won't blow up into anything big."

"You sure?"

"They pissed me off. Once they know I'm pissed off, they'll back off."

Sano went on and on, apologizing in Kurauchi's stead.

I stood next to the fish tank for a while after I got off the phone. I was still pissed off.

I stuck my hand in the water.

I managed to grab the goldfish, quick as he was. He was still trying to swim, squirming in the palm of my hand. I slowly tightened my grip.

He stopped moving. I held still for a moment, and then squeezed again. I felt something—the fish, of course—crushing in my hand. A soft mound of flesh. I squeezed again. It was crushed. Something came spilling out of my fist.

Its intestines spilled out of its mouth and rear. I kept squeezing, as if I was trying to squeeze the last drops of water from a damp towel. Its intestines floated about in the water, like something strange. Where the bubbles spewed forth, the entrails danced busily.

I didn't let go of the fish's stringy corpse for a while.

I took my hand out of the water. It felt numb.

"See what happens when a punk tries to turn cartwheels? Don't ever think you can get out."

I started to light a cigarette, but stopped and threw the Dupont in the water. It made a funny sound and got tangled with the fish intestines before sinking to the bottom.

I tried not to think about anything. I focused my energy on the pain in my side.

"Punks shouldn't think about getting out. Punks got to stay in their place." The words came tumbling out. I had to get rid of the habit, that was certain.

The phone rang and my body jolted. It felt like someone else's body. I reached for the phone, my hand still wet.

"It's Sugimoto." He sounded slightly out of breath.

"What's up?"

"It's done. I admit it wasn't an easy thing to do."

"Another reason why I really had to get hurt."

"I'll have Mutoh give himself up, in the morning."

"Sorry about that."

"Now they owe us a big favor, the main family."

"That's what it comes down to."

"Okay then." Sugimoto was about to hang up.

"So..."

"What is it, Boss?"

"Well, so, you took care of it all. You took care of everything."

"Yes, I did." Sugimoto didn't wait for my response and hung up.

I stared at the floating intestines in the fish tank. The goldfish that did flips was gone.

# BATHING

## 1

I was cleaning.

Strangely enough, I didn't mind it. It was a moldy old place in an apartment complex, but I'd been living here for twelve years. From the time I was thirty. During the two years I spent behind bars, Ayumi came around from time to time and cleaned the place. The first of those terms lasted a year and a half, and the other six months. I don't know what would have happened to my place if Ayumi hadn't been around. The remaining six years I served in my twenties. I went in twice—five years, and then one year. The five years was for knocking off a civilian. I spent more than half my twenties on the inside.

I vacuumed carefully in between the tatami mats and wiped down the areas I couldn't reach with the vacuum using a damp cloth. I used a dry cloth on the sideboard.

It had become so routine that no matter how carefully I went about cleaning, I didn't waste any energy. At most, it only took two hours to do my two-bedroom apartment.

I didn't clean to kill time. I'd done my share of that—enough to make me sick—while I was behind bars.

And it wasn't as if I had all that much free time, anyway. I was in the middle of trying to double the number of drug routes. We were trying to expand in collection and real estate, too. With the work I'd given Yoshie, her girls had grown to three times the number she began with. The number of times I had to yell into the phone increased, too.

As for the war, it was over, for now. In the end, the rival gangs weren't able to take advantage of the Boss's illness. It was because I'd planned things pretty well. That's what I thought, at least.

We didn't have to sacrifice any people during the war, but the main family's beams were rotting. It was because Kurauchi made others handle everything and never stood at the forefront of anything. Kurauchi hadn't taken over the Clan yet. He'd taken a wrong turn. If he'd stood his ground, he'd have taken over by now. It was definitely over for the Boss; he was too sick to recover.

I was the one who'd stood my ground, I who was forced to branch out. But guys came over to my gang, and now we were more than twenty. Compared to that, the main family, which had once numbered fifty, was now down to about thirty. And all that had happened in the space of three months.

I put away the vacuum cleaner and tossed out the bucket of water. Then I began polishing the glassware in the sideboard. I didn't mind doing that either. It was a good feeling to pour whiskey into a sparkling clean glass.

The phone rang.

It was Sugimoto with some information. He was working on adding new drug routes. Because Kurauchi had knocked down the main family's share of the profits to just a half, he was feeling things out to see if we'd be willing to give back the routes we'd borrowed from them. It wasn't a firm demand. He couldn't make any claims on me right now. But I had announced at the officers' meeting that if the Clan was in dire financial straits, we'd give back what we'd been entrusted with.

But just giving something back wasn't the *yakuza* way. You doubled the number of routes, kept the new ones, and gave back the old. You lured the cops into focusing on the old routes. Eventually they'd find some incriminating evidence. The cops didn't care if a route was new or old; all they wanted were the points they earned for a drug bust.

And our time was almost up.

After I got off the phone with Sugimoto, I resumed polishing the glassware. Sugimoto wasn't opposed to my living here. But whenever other members came around, I used Ayumi's apartment in Shibuya. No one liked to think that their boss was living in some shitty apartment complex.

I finished polishing, making sure I didn't leave any fingerprints on the glasses, and put them all back in the sideboard one by one.

I always did the cleaning and the laundry by myself. The only thing I didn't do was cook. That was about it. Strangely enough, I didn't really think about food. I never tired of eating the same thing for days. My kitchen was always clean and I didn't own many pots and pans. I didn't even have expired groceries in my refrigerator. In fact, I cleaned it out once every three days.

The phone rang again. It was Ayumi. Ever since she started her club in Akasaka, *Club Lisa*, she called me often for instructions. Things were different from when she used to run the old place, with just her and a bartender. She wasn't as free to run things the way she pleased anymore.

"I think it's about time you collected."

It was concerning a bill four months overdue. She'd tried to collect, even going as far as visiting the guy's office, but each time he made empty promises. We were talking four hundred thousand yen. Ayumi wasn't used to collecting on debts yet. Her previous businesses had all been cash only.

"I need something more on this guy."

"I got something. You know that girl Emi? He slept with her, and she's involved somehow."

"When? How many times did he sleep with her?"

"Twice. She used to work at the old place."

"I got it. Keep Emi out of sight for a while."

I got off the phone, smirking. Handling the kind of business best left to the young ones. Sugimoto wouldn't like it. I decided to go it alone.

I gave myself a close shave, and got dressed in a clean shirt and suit. I never permed my hair, nor ever wore snappy black suits and gold bracelets. I couldn't care less about what belt buckle or watch I wore. I couldn't stand guys who bothered with fashion.

I left the apartment, taking a bus and then a train to get to where the guy's office was.

I found the building right away. The office took up the entire fourth floor. It was the only business in the place. I opened the door to find only ten employees. It had to be a privately-owned company. It'd be easy to put the squeeze on this place, if I wanted to.

I headed for the door at the back, not even bothering to consult the receptionist. One of the employees looked up with curiosity. I knocked. A deep voice answered.

"A pleasure. I'm Tanaka."

"Look here, I can't have you barging in to the place like this. Didn't anyone say anything to you?"

"You must be Taniuchi-san." I closed the door behind me. He was in his fifties and had a ruddy complexion.

"I'm here about your *Club Lisa* account."

"What, to collect? I told that old hag to hold off."

Ayumi was only thirty-one, too young for anyone to call her an old hag. It was always the guys who hadn't paid up who took that kind of familiar tone.

"I don't really know the manager of that place. I don't even know how much you owe."

"So how are you expecting to collect?"

"Well, to tell you the truth, there's some girl who took on your debts. Taniuchi-san, you were a customer of a girl called Emi, right?"

Taniuchi's expression changed slightly.

I put a cigarette in my mouth and lit it. "Emi took out a loan to pay off your debt. How should we put it? She didn't borrow from the nicest people. They told her to go work it off in a Soapland brothel."

"It's four hundred thousand, right? I'll pay up."

"No, it's four million."

"What the hell?"

"Emi borrowed four million."

"What I owed was four hundred thousand. The rest of it isn't my problem."

"Emi said that to pay off your debt, she borrowed four million. She's asking that you pay it off for her. I get two percent. So that's eighty thousand."

"It should really be just eight thousand, you know. I can pay you that much right now. Anyway, get out of here. I'm busy."

"There's a bunch of guys who'll do it for forty percent of the share. But they aren't the type who'll come knocking at your door, all nice like I did. If I leave empty-handed, Emi'll ask those guys to do it. They'll make you pay up—all four million—somehow or other."

"Can't pull nothing out of nothing, you know. You're actually in a good position when you haven't got the money."

"But you've got this company. They'll come after your company. And if you have a house, that too. Well, my part's over. So you're not going to give me anything. There aren't many people who realize in time that it's so much better to work through me. It's all over for you if those guys show up here."

"I have an advisory lawyer, you know. We can fight the *yakuza* with the law."

"They've got lawyers, too. Lawyers who're used to this kind of thing. Let me give you a piece of advice. Just give them exactly what they ask for as soon as they ask for it. Otherwise it'll snowball into something you can't handle, and you'll need nerves of steel to put up with what they'll do to you." I ground out my cigarette and got up. It was a stupid man who didn't ask me to stay at that point. Really, the damage wouldn't stop at four million.

"If you'll excuse me," I said.

"Wait a minute. How much time do I have to give it to you?"

"Your time's up. You have to hand it over right now."

"You think I can get that kind of cash so easily?"

"You got no choice. Mine's a one-time proposition. Whether or not you pay up on time depends on how lucky you are."

"Can you make a living on just two percent?"

"There are guys who owe money in Akasaka, and Ginza too. I only have to make one visit, so it's no big deal. And I don't usually get requests like Emi's. It's usually a question of five or six hundred thousand. It's only a couple of times a year that I get a request for four million."

"Not four million. Four hundred thousand."

There was a sharp edge to Taniuchi's tone. Had it been four hundred thousand, he probably would have paid out of hand. But I'd decided it would be four million. Four million because I had to come all the way to his office. That was my only reason.

I bowed and walked out. Taniuchi didn't try to stop me.

2

At the office, Sugimoto was shouting into the phone. There were six young guys there, and the scene gave off the impression of an up-and-coming gang.

"Did you come out by yourself again, Boss?" Sugimoto said, putting down the phone.

"When can we return the main family's drug routes?"

"Tomorrow. In my opinion, I think it would be better if we gave it back sooner rather than later. The cops are already in pretty deep. Plus they don't have a clue about our new routes."

"So why don't we call the main family. Kurauchi's probably straining his neck looking out for us."

The Boss's condition kept fluctuating. If things went on like this, he'd find himself an old man before he could recover. He hadn't decided on his successor. There was still the belief going around that Kurauchi would be the center of things, but he'd lost a man during the war.

"I'm going out. I have to get out to the site. I got a lot of things I have to take care of."

"Don't do anything rash, Sugimoto. We can't afford to have you behind bars."

"I know." Sugimoto bowed and left.

I sat around in the office for a while, staring off into space. Three desks. Two sofas and four chairs. The place seated ten. It was fine when we first started off, but the place wasn't big enough anymore. It wasn't a bad location, right near Meguro station. The sign outside read "Tanaka Goods, Ltd." so passers-by had no way of knowing that it was really a *yakuza* headquarters.

"We'll soon overtake the main family. We've got to. I don't work the way Kurauchi does," I muttered. I was trying to be more careful about talking to myself, but I couldn't help myself when I wasn't paying close attention. One of the younger guys was staring at me.

"Munakata," I called, and he answered loudly, jumping up from the sofa. Since we'd sent Mutoh off to do time, Munakata was the most reliable of the junior members.

"You free?"

"For now. Brother told us to stand by."

There were six men at the office.

"It's a tough job. Take two or three guys with you. I'll explain things to Sugimoto."

"We going to break some windows or something?"

"This isn't war. If we can manage to avoid fighting, that's the best. For us, having Mutoh behind bars is difficult enough."

"So what's this tough job, then?"

"You'll be dealing with a civilian. Make sure you don't hurt him. Otherwise the cops'll get involved. Also, don't let them find out who did it." I wrote the name and address of Takeuchi's company on a piece of paper and handed it to Munakata.

"They deal in women's clothing. Disrupt their business for a few days. Make sure no one sees your faces. And be careful of the cops."

"Disrupt their business? How bad do you want things messed up?"

"See how it goes. I'll leave it up to you. Make sure he starts wondering if it might not go on forever."

"I get it."

Munakata left, taking two of the junior members with him. Compared to Mutoh, there was something underhanded about him. If you were going to send someone off to prison—someone who'd go without much fuss—Mutoh was your man, but Munakata was the one you wanted for a job like this.

I pretty much knew the score when it came to the guys I brought with me from the main family. It was the new guys that I hadn't figured out yet. *Yakuza* folk tended to be nonstandard. It took time to really understand one. You had to see him in many different kinds of situations.

I sat there for a while, staring at the legitimate business ledger in front of me. Tanaka Goods, Ltd., distributed hot towels and various dried food snacks to the bars in our territory. The kickbacks we demanded from them didn't appear in Tanaka Goods' account books.

We'd originally been given just a tiny part of the main family's turf, so we didn't do business with that many bars. To begin with, we were no longer living in the hot towel days. I couldn't support our whole gang on that kind of income, but I arranged things so that we had two employees working for Tanaka Goods, Ltd. I figured the police would feel more comfortable if we, as *yakuza*, did the kind of business that *yakuza* had always done. And it gave a needed sense of stability to the young members.

I wasn't the type to keep tabs on the accounts. I wouldn't understand them even if I looked them over. What made me keep accounts even then was my seeing the Boss get out of trouble numerous times thanks to the records he kept. He didn't have to pay taxes, it looked as if he was running a legitimate business, and banks had approved him for loans.

Sugimoto's high school buddy was our bookkeeper; he'd been ruined by gambling debts. He had a first-class accounting license. We couldn't leave him in charge of our black market income, but Sugimoto and I decided that he could handle our legitimate earnings. On the condition that we made sure he understood what it meant to be *yakuza.*

"Yoshimoto, any progress with that matter we discussed?"

The young guy who'd just returned from his rounds was Yoshino, a college graduate who'd lived in America to boot. He came on his own to the office, looking for work. I still found his behavior somewhat suspicious. I took him to Ayumi's bar a number of times and drank with him, but he kept harping obsessively on how he wanted to manage a roulette parlor.

"Frankly, I think *yakuza*-run gambling is old hat," Yoshino said.

"If you can't do what you've been asked to do, get out. Don't forget you aren't even a member of the family."

"All right, I know. Anyhow, I've located groups of gambling aficionados and I'm getting to know them. I think we should be nice to the richer shopkeepers, who have the money to play at roulette."

"All we need to do is make sure they never lose too big."

"And forget about roulette?"

"I'm still thinking about it."

We needed a lot of capital. Once we had that, everything else would be smooth sailing. A couple of gambling houses that would bring in big money. That should give us capital. Roulette, poker, dice. It didn't matter what. Go beyond that, and the police wanted to talk to you. We'd have to worry about the cops cracking down on everything else, too.

"Yoshino, to do business, you need to do serious market research. It's not as simple as just opening up a gambling joint. What's going to make or break us is getting customers."

"It's just as you say."

"So what about the job I gave you."

"Okay. But I get too into it myself when I start thinking about roulette. It's my dream to run a roulette parlor."

"Yeah, you keep saying. Better not be taking down the customers' phone numbers in your pocket book."

"I'm scrambling the numbers. If I get caught, I'll swallow the chart."

"You got to be prepared to do time if you're going to handle gambling operations."

"I only hope it comes after I've been offered a place in the family."

"You gotta earn that sort of thing."

Yoshino lowered his head to say he understood.

I listened for about an hour to Yoshino's gambling ideas. Once in a while you came across a guy who was less interested in betting than in seeing others bet. As far as gambling went, I could leave it all to him. The question was how far I could trust him with other things. Now was my chance to find out. I had to put him in charge of something other than gambling—to see if he would foresake his god for the gang. In our world such tests were commonplace.

Sugimoto called twice. I let him know I was using
Munakata for another job and sent the other guys over to
Sugimoto. It seems he'd pretty much taken care of the drug
routes.

Things were busy. If I came out to the office, there was
always something that needed doing. Especially now, since
I had my own gang and we were trying to catch the rising
tide.

"It's like I'm the president of some little company." I
was talking to myself. I was trying to be careful, but I could-
n't help myself. One of the guys got up off the sofa,
thinking I'd said something to him.

"Go on the rounds, will you? Don't go sticking your
nose in anything. We can't afford having the cops on our
tail right now."

They left, leaving just one behind. Sugimoto had probably issued orders to have at least one guy always stay
behind to cover me, just in case. The main family's war
wasn't entirely over yet. They could still rub me out, and
that would turn the tables.

"Hey. How old're you?" I called out to the guy, who
stiffened.

"Nineteen, sir."

I tried to recall his name, but it didn't come to me right
away. I remembered his telling me once before that he was
nineteen. He was some punk that Sugimoto had picked up
in town.

"You'll never make it as a *yakuza* if you go into it

half-assed."

"Yes."

"We *yakuza* are people that society rejected, who've huddled together to survive by hook or by crook. Sometimes a guy will have to give up his life to help his buddy. And maybe someone will have to give up his life for you, too."

"I'm no use to anyone. All I can do is give up my life for someone else."

"Well don't go throwing it away. I'll tell you when it's time to make the sacrifice." As I spoke, I realized I sounded exactly like the Boss. I too was nineteen when I first met the Boss. And for more than twenty years, the Boss had used me for whatever purpose suited him.

"Our time's coming. You're looking at a man of experience."

"I'm willing to do anything. If you need a hit man, I'm here."

We hadn't made him a member of our clan yet. He was still trying to earn his badge, so to speak. I wasn't the type to offer it to just anybody. And if people knew that, then the offer would be worth more when it was made.

Sugimoto was working his fingers to the bone to expand our gang. However, in another ten years, he'd probably want his own gang. The Boss, too, had no other alternative but to break up his gang, giving a branch each to three younger brothers. I was one of his children, so my case was different. The former younger brothers' pay-off to him was a bare minimum, just what was dictated by obligation.

Sugimoto served now as my junior boss, but originally he'd been one of my younger brothers. He deserved the same kind of privilege someday. It was a question of how much I could get out of him until then.

I stared down at the accounts, useless as that was.

Sugimoto returned, bringing five of the juniors with him.

I got three new pieces of information regarding the drug routes. We had to return the old routes to the main family as soon as possible. There was traffic along the new routes already, much more than on the old routes.

"I'm going home."

"Boss, how about getting yourself a Mercedes one of these days?"

"No, Sugimoto. You're not supposed to stand out until you have real power, got it? Our gang's already got three cars. That's enough for now. I know a *yakuza*'s got to look good. But when the Clan Boss is sick, I can't go around riding in a Mercedes."

"I'm sorry. It's just that the drug routes are doing so well right now. I got carried away."

It wasn't really that Sugimoto wanted me to drive a Mercedes. But the children wanted it. And sometimes he had to let me know what was up.

"I'm going to meet with Sano Brother. I'll let you know the details tomorrow."

When we got outside, I whispered to Sugimoto. Sugimoto nodded and opened the back door to the car. One of the young guys was driving.

It was just your average domestic car. That was good enough for now. We'd get a Mercedes once we surpassed the main family. The younger guys'd be pretty damn excited then. Sugimoto shut the door with a little gesture of deference.

## 3

Sano was already there.

It was a small place, with just one bartender, located in some generic building in Shibuya. It'd been there for twenty years, and Sano and some other of my brothers used to take me there often for drinks.

"So you're giving back the old drug routes to Kurauchi."

"I'm giving it back to the main family, not Kurauchi."

"That means, to Kurauchi. He lowered the rates himself, but then decided he wasn't making enough off you, so he wants the routes back. He doesn't work like a *yakuza*, does he."

"But he'll owe me one. After all, they're hard up for cash now."

"The place is falling apart. To think that a guy who

can't even stand at the head during war is calling the shots! If you weren't helping them out, they'd have been crushed by now."

There'd always been bad blood between Sano and Kurauchi. Sano and I got along well, and there'd been a time when he thought that I'd be taking over eventually. After I'd been made to branch off, his plans had gone to pot.

In terms of rank in *yakuza* society, he wasn't quite my big brother. He was the Boss's younger brother, so he was more like an Uncle to me. But if you had been in the same gang, you called him Brother.

If I had taken over the main family, he would have been like my guardian. He'd have been called Boss, but he wouldn't have had any children. In our society, you often found such gang leaders. If Kurauchi were to succeed the Boss, Sano might retain his current title of proxy, but things would be very different. It'd be hard for him there, and he'd surely have to retire.

Unlike the other Uncles, Sano didn't have what it takes to start up a gang. The reason was simple: he hadn't lived his life preparing for it.

"The war isn't over," I said. "If we show them any sign of weakness, they'll come after us again."

"Kurauchi knows it, too. But what he's after is money. He thinks if he hoards enough dough, he'll win wars too."

"That's a problem."

"And there's no way you can go back to the main family,

after you've branched out."

"How's the Boss doing?"

"It's curtains for him. You got to wonder how he even made it this far. He never made it clear who his successor's going to be either. Not once. I bet Kurauchi's just going to take over naturally, since he's the junior boss."

In other words, the eldest son would take over the family business. That was the custom.

I requested another whiskey and lit a cigarette.

When and where to push. That was the question. And whether or not there was still any ambition as a *yakuza* left in Sano's heart. It was a gamble I had to take.

"How old are you now, Brother Sano?"

"Fifty-one. Almost fifty-two."

"Will you let me call you Uncle at least once?"

Sano had begun to raise his glass to his lips but paused halfway. He stared at me. I blew out a cloud of smoke and put the lit cigarette in the ashtray.

"You asking me to get my own gang together?"

"A part of me wants you to stay with the main family. But since I can't possibly be the one who'll be taking over, I won't be able to do anything for you if you stay over there."

"And if I form my own gang?"

"In that case, I think I could help you out. It'd be a relationship between branch bosses, so I wouldn't be butting into the main family's affairs by helping you."

"Hey, Tanaka, watch what you're saying."

I ground out the cigarette in the ashtray. "I know I shouldn't be saying these things while the Boss's still alive. But it'll be too late after he's dead.  You won't be getting a single thing from the Boss once he's gone. When really you're entitled to over half."

"Oh, not me."

"You mean you're not sure you can do it. Don't get angry at me for saying this. We've known each other for more than twenty years, and I feel like I know you pretty well. No one really has the confidence. No one thinks he can really handle things. Look at Kurauchi. He doesn't know his ass from his elbow. If he'd had the chance, the Boss'd have offered you a gang of your own, Brother. But he went on the defensive. He wanted to give you what you deserved, but he became conservative and suspicious. Knowing that, you chose to be patient."

"Still, Tanaka. I don't know about what you're suggesting."

"If Kawano wants to make a gang, it'd mean breaking up a family. But who'd complain if you did, Sano Brother. You could even argue that you're trying to make things easier for Kurauchi by bowing out. I can see it."

"See what?"

"How you're going to be treated after the Boss's gone. Kurauchi's not going to pay any attention to guardianship or anything. And the other Uncles, they're not going to get involved. Just look at what happened during the war."

Sano put a cigarette in his mouth. I offered him a light.

"I thought I'd have to retire."

"But you got a nice young wife just yesterday, and your kids have just started elementary school. What about them? A guy who's put in thirty years as a *yakuza* doesn't have too many career options."

"That's true."

"And it's not as if you saved up your earnings."

"So what are you saying? Are you offering to take care of me in my old age?"

"Well that's taking it too far. But I want to be able to call you Uncle, because that's what you really are to me. I couldn't have made it this far without you."

"I can't really become your gang's guardian…"

"Brother, that'd be a big loss of face for Kurauchi."

"That's true."

I lit another cigarette. Sano wasn't even flicking the ashes off his.

If Sano said he was branching out, there was no way Kurauchi could refuse. Sano would probably only take about three men with him, but it would still be a big blow to the main family. It would be a sign to both insiders and outsiders that the main family was in decline.

"Please think about it, Brother—no, Uncle."

I didn't push him any more than that, and got up. The bartender bowed his head slightly. Nothing much had changed in twenty years.

I got outside and hailed a cab. I'd already sent home the car.

"Shinjuku."

After I spoke, I realized with surprise that I was in a good mood. Not that there was anything wrong with that. I lit up, and the taxi driver objected. I kept smoking, ignoring his request. The driver pulled over to the left side of the road and turned around.

"I'm sorry, sir, but I don't smoke."

"Yeah? Well I do."

"Then please smoke somewhere else. You can pay the fare as far as here."

"Well I'm sorry about that. But I smoke where I want, when I want. I can't change my habits now. Just drive on quietly, like a good man. Don't get me upset."

"I don't want to breathe your second-hand smoke. Please, get out."

"I'm warning you. Don't make me mad."

"I don't want to get lung cancer."

"You're not getting lung cancer right this second, are you? But if you force me out now, you're going to die."

He clicked his tongue in annoyance and started driving. He was driving pretty rough. I was in disbelief over my own patience with the guy. I lit up another cigarette. The driver opened up a window. I didn't do anything; I just kept smoking.

The cab stopped and the door opened for me. "Lucky you! You had a close brush with death back there," I marveled, accepting the change. He didn't even look at me.

"What's wrong with me?" I muttered, walking along

the street.

"He was lucky. Like he got a second chance at life." The habit again. It wasn't going to be easy to break it. I pushed open the door to the bar. I scanned the place for Yoko.

"Welcome back, Tanaka-san!" Yoko stood up from a corner booth. "You don't look so good."

"The cabbie told me I couldn't smoke in his car."

"That so? He should put a big sign on his cab saying NO SMOKING."

Yoko grabbed my wrist and pulled me over to a seat. It was my fourth time here. Last time I took her out after closing, and we went for a drink. She probably would have come with me to a hotel if I'd asked, but I just escorted her home.

I sat down and they brought over my private bottle. It was still more than half-full. I ordered some cheese and fruit.

"It's expensive. Don't go out of your way for me," Yoko whispered.

I was being overly solicitous of her feelings. I think I was trying to show off.

She was just a twenty-one year old girl, like any other. Seeing her in a place like this, though, it was obvious she wasn't a total amateur. Sometimes I wondered what she was really after. But whenever I saw her smiling face, I was dazzled. Senselessly dazzled.

I didn't really have anything to say, we just made small talk. I sipped at my drink until closing, and then I took

Yoko out again.

"Tanaka-san, you're not really single, are you?"

We went outside and Yoko put her arm in mine. Even that little gesture made my heart beat faster.

"I can't lie to a woman."

"Last time, you didn't even ask if you could come in. You just went home."

"There's no one waiting for me at home."

"I thought you were lying. I thought you were going home to your wife after we said goodbye."

"I live alone. If you don't believe me, why don't you come by?"

"Really?"

It meant the same as inviting her to a hotel. Actually, it meant a little more. Whether it was a hotel or not, it amounted to the same thing: *I* was inviting *her*. Force them. Take them. That was all there was to it. There was a time when I did all that in dark alleys.

Yoko hailed a cab. She got in but didn't tell the driver where we were going.

"Kitasuna," I said. I didn't feel like going to some hotel.

I didn't talk during the trip. We just sat there, our fingers intertwined. From time to time I felt a slight pressure from Yoko's fingers. I'd never done anything like that even with Ayumi, whom I'd known for over ten years.

I could see the apartment complex. I told the driver where to turn. "Right there."

The car stopped. I paid and accepted the change. It hit

me that I hadn't even craved a cigarette in the time it took us to get here from Shinjuku.

We went up the stairs. The sound of footsteps. It was different from usual. In between the sound of my footsteps was the clicking of Yoko's high heels. She seemed uncomfortable. Maybe she was starting to feel nervous.

We went inside. It was neat as always, of course. The light shone coldly over the room. Yoko looked around as if she were searching for something. Signs of another woman. She wouldn't find anything.

I put my jacket on a hanger and pulled my tie loose. Yoko sat down in a chair in the dining area.

"Do you want a drink?"

"I'll do it, Tanaka-san."

"This is my place. You sit." I got some ice from the freezer and made two on the rocks.

"I thought your place would be more messy than this. Like your dishes would be all piled up in the sink, and there'd be dust all over your furniture."

"When you live on your own for a long time, you pick up certain habits."

"Tanaka-san, how come you never got married?"

"There are some questions I'd rather not answer."

"I'm sorry."

Seems Yoko misunderstood. She brought her glass of on the rocks to her lips, fluttering her eyelashes.

Of course there was any number of *yakuza* who got hitched, even put their names on the family register with a woman. Somehow I never did, and that was all there was to it.

I drew a bath and laid out a futon in the six-mat tatami room. The show was over; I wasn't going to go out of my way for her. I'd have her. I was going back to my old ways.

"It has to be someone like you for me. I'm not into those younger guys."

"Yeah? Well I prefer young women."

I smoked a cigarette and sipped my drink. Ayumi was always nagging me that drinking made me impotent when really it was Ayumi who made me impotent.

The tiny bathtub filled up quickly.

I urged Yoko to take a bath, and she went over to the bathroom without much fuss.

Listening to the splashing water, I smoked another cigarette. It didn't take long for her to come out. She was wrapped up in a towel.

I pushed her into the room where I had the futon laid out. I'd have this girl. But I didn't feel like it anymore.

"Please be gentle. I don't like it rough," she said, after I pushed her down.

Keeping a woman loyal through sex. It wouldn't be my first time. But nor was I the kind who had pearls inserted in his penis in prison. Mood. Maybe that's what you'd call it. The moment I decided to make money by putting a woman to work, I became a different man.

Her body still had something virginal about it. The way she moved, her faint moans. She hadn't reached sexual maturity yet. When I tried to enter her, she screamed and protested. But her body wasn't refusing me.

How much could this girl earn? That's what was on my mind.

4

Kurauchi and I met, as equals.

If Kurauchi weren't the closest thing to the Boss's official designate, it could have been sixty-forty, but I acknowledged his position and requested a fifty-fifty meeting.

Since I was going to all that trouble, I requested that Uncles Ohyama and Mizuta preside over the meeting. Maybe it was going a bit overboard for the drug routes that I'd been entrusted with, but for me, and for Kurauchi too, it had the merit of making our position and relationship very clear.

But, as it turned out, it felt more like a sixty-forty, or even a seventy-thirty situation. I was giving them their routes back because the main family was having financial difficulties. Kurauchi was probably relieved, but he must have been boiling on the inside at the same time.

Once everything was settled, the people on the job would handle the rest. I had to treat the two Uncles to a nice meal. Both Ohyama and Mizuta had gangs of their own, with about thirty men each. Both were the plodding type. During a war, they'd send over just one or two of their own men as a token of loyalty. The other Uncle, Harada, was in danger of ruin. The Boss was never inclined to lend him a hand. Harada had opened up a gambling business with a lot of fanfare and managed to destroy himself without any outside assistance. He himself was doing time and wasn't getting out of prison for another three years.

"So Kurauchi, what's going on with Sano?" Ohyama asked. Both Ohyama and Mizuta preferred fish to meat. Or to be precise, they loved red snapper. The red snapper on each man's plate was now mostly just bones.

"Sano Brother seems to be considering various options."

"He's thinking of getting together his own gang, isn't he? Why don't you give him what you can? It was out of consideration for Brother"—meaning the Clan Boss—"that Sano never went after a gang for himself. You guys call him Brother, but he's really supposed to be your Uncle."

"I understand, absolutely."

Kurauchi was asking Sano to put a hold on getting together his own gang. But Sano was trying to force the issue. Kurauchi probably thought that once he was officially the Clan Boss designate, he could easily stop Sano.

"Sano Brother's trying to start up his own business, is he?" I asked Kurauchi. I pretended not to know anything, but in fact I even knew how many Sano would take with him: four.

"That's the word."

"If you want to know the truth, he ought to have had his own gang before I did."

"I was planning to ask him to be guardian."

"Since that's what the Boss had in mind too. And the Boss won't be changing his mind, in his current state. Kurauchi-san, you're trying to be loyal to the Boss's will, right?"

"That's right."

"Makes sense too because a branching move by Sano Brother right now would shake the main family."

"Uncles Ohyama and Mizuta, and you, too, Tanaka Brother, have agreed to think of me as the Clan Boss designate. How I treat Sano Brother is a question of face for the main family." As he spoke, his mouth twitched with annoyance. He was really pissed off. He must have been praying hard that the Boss, sleeping away in the hospital, would just hurry up and die so he could finally take over. His position was ambiguous, and had remained ambiguous for too long; he was being pecked at by everyone. That's how things stood for Kurauchi.

He had gotten back the drug routes. That was his lifeline at the moment. But he didn't know when the police would find out and when they'd interfere. I returned the routes no poorer than they were when I had received them; but in the space of just three months, the police were sniffing all over them. Of course the responsibility was seen to be Kurauchi's, since the change had taken place after I had given them back.

"Hey, Tanaka, things are going pretty well with you, I hear."

"Well, Ohyama Uncle, we're right out on the front lines of the war. If we went down, they'd attack the whole Clan again. I gotta at least put up a strong front."

"Yeah, I got you. I'm not trying to pick a fight or anything. I think Brother did a good thing in having you set up your own family."

When it came to the subject of wars, the Uncles couldn't really butt in. They couldn't, really, unless they were ready to put themselves on the line to defend the main family.

"We've got to start all over again with our drug routes. Got to wind up the young guys again," I said.

"Well, I must say, you've got the main family's best interests at heart," Kurauchi replied.

Our dinner meeting was coming to an end.

Sugimoto was probably going to go all out with our new drug routes tomorrow. We were using the old routes as shields to dodge the bullets, and things were probably safer now than they'd ever been.

"Once things are settled with Sano Brother, it might be a good idea to get things settled over here about who's taking over. It's not really my place to stick my nose in, as someone who's branched off, so I'm asking Uncles Ohyama and Mizuta to take care of things." As far as

Ohyama and Mizuta were concerned, they couldn't completely ignore Sano's wishes when it came to deciding who the successor was going to be. If Sano didn't want to be Kurauchi's guardian, there was no other alternative but to grant him his own gang.

Kurauchi and I stood next to each other as we saw off Ohyama and Mizuta. My men and the main family's all lined up behind us.

"I'm going to be the next Clan Boss, right, Tanaka Brother?"

"What, you think we were all lying when we showed support?"

"I want to be the Clan Boss both in name and in reality. The challenge is how not to be swallowed up by the Tanaka gang."

"Well, I gotta feed my guys somehow, Kurauchi-san. I'll do what I have to."

"That makes two of us. It isn't bad to have a little competition, but I never thought your gang'd grow so big before I even took over the Clan."

"Me neither. I was prepared to perish in that war."

Our car came around. I got in my nondescript domestic car and Kurauchi in his black Mercedes. It had just been polished and gave off a sharp glint even at night.

I took our young men to Ayumi's bar in Akasaka. The guys were depressed, on account of Kurauchi's Mercedes. They were starting to think that the main family was after all the main family. I had to take them out for a good night's drinking to make them forget.

Ayumi said to me, "Taniuchi called for you twice yesterday. He wanted to know how to get in touch with you. So I told him I didn't know, and to contact Emi. Emi hasn't gone back to her apartment, so I'm sure he's having a tough time of it. He asked me to tell you he wants you to call."

"So what does Emi think? I mean, about squeezing dough out of him."

"I'm sure she's liking it. She could never stand his stinginess."

"Good. We're almost there. Anyway, show my boys a good time and let them drink. I'll give him a call."

Seems Munakata did a good job. I had him put in a dunning call, saying pay up or else. But we hadn't specified the amount.

It wasn't as though he owed money for a legitimate loan. He'd just signed a voucher saying that he'd be responsible for Emi's debts. That was all.

I took a stool over to the phone in the corner and sat down. I had the voucher he'd signed in my possession. Taniuchi, of course, believed that it was in Emi's possession, since she was the one who'd borrowed money to pay for his bill for *Club Lisa*.

It must have been a direct line to his office, because Taniuchi picked up.

"This is Tanaka calling. I came by some time ago about the bill for *Club Lisa*."

"Ahh, Tanaka-san."

"I just happened to run into *Club Lisa's Mama-san*. She said you wanted to talk to me?"

"I'll pay it. Four million. I've got no alternative. I'll pay it."

"Pardon me?"

"You know, about Emi's bill. We talked about it. I might as well be throwing it down a hole, but I have no choice."

"Is this some bad joke? I'm not on that case anymore. I told you when I spoke to you last that it was a one-time proposition."

"I'm willing to pay the four million, to Emi. Four million! How could you refuse it?"

"Well, if you had said all of this when I saw you, I'd have accepted it gladly."

"Anyway, will you contact Emi? And tell her to make them stop."

"What is Emi doing?"

"They're staining the merchandise. They're getting my transportation vans involved in all sorts of accidents before they even get to the boutiques. They're causing trouble at the boutiques. Retailers are starting to cancel their orders."

"Emi's not making them do that. She just asked someone else to take care of the accounts. They're the ones who're doing it. Didn't you get a phone call reminding you to pay up?"

"Just once. They didn't say how much."

"Well that's a problem. Didn't I warn you?"

"It is a problem. It's terrible. I want to take care of things as speedily as possible."

"I think that'll be impossible."

"Anyway, you can get in touch with Emi, can't you? Tell her I'll pay the four million."

"Four million won't be enough. They didn't tell you how much you owed, did they? It's because they want to get more than four million out of you."

"But what I owe is really just four hundred thousand, give or take. Who does business like this? They don't even have written proof."

Taniuchi was getting really upset now. Here was a guy who didn't want to pay his bill for four hundred thousand, and now he was eager to pay four million. Munakata must've done a smashing good job.

"They might not have something in writing, but you did sign the bill at *Club Lisa*, didn't you? The moment Emi shouldered those debts, the bill passed on to her. It has the same validity as a voucher."

"That's why I'm saying I'm willing to pay the four million."

"You don't understand. I already said I don't have anything to do with it anymore. If you had paid me the four million when I saw you, everything would have been squared away. Even if all Emi wants is the four million, the guys who are doing the work for her are going to try to squeeze every last bit out of you. It's terrible."

"How much do I have to pay to take care of this?"

"I don't know. Don't ask me. How much are you willing to pay?"

"Four million five hundred thousand."

He really was stingy. I laughed quietly.

"But if you include the damage to my merchandise, that would be a loss of seven million right there."

"I wouldn't know about that. What I know is that you didn't want to pay the four hundred thousand at first, and so the sum ballooned to four million. And then you wouldn't pay the four million, so now you're in this position. You better think it over. Well, it's not any of my business anymore."

"I've notified the police."

"Have they done anything?"

Taniuchi didn't answer. What he was to the police was some guy who owed people some money.

"Well, I can get in touch with Emi for you. I might be able to find out who's doing the work for her. But I can't very well tell you who the people are."

"Can you ask her, ask Emi? Ask her how much she wants."

"What Emi wants is four million. She wants four million, every yen of it. I can understand that, don't you too? You not only used her, but had her take on a debt of four hundred thousand yen. But there are ways to get at people who don't want to pay up, and those guys whom she asked, well, they know how. If you had paid up what you owed, it never would have come to this. They never would have gotten involved."

Taniuchi didn't say anything for a while. I lit a cigarette. The three young guys, surrounded by girls, were having a good time.

"Can you do anything to help me out, Tanaka-san?"

"I warned you, didn't I? That they'd come after your business. Taniuchi-san, do you have family?"

"That's irrelevant."

"Of course it's relevant. You're the one who played around and didn't pay the bill, and that's your responsibility, but because of you, they'll lose the family breadwinner."

"How much do they want? How much do I need to pay?"

"Please don't keep asking me. Anyway, I'll try and get a hold of Emi for you."

I hung up.

"So how much d'you think we'll get?" Ayumi came over and asked. I thought I could get about ten million, but I didn't tell her. It wasn't a woman's business to know.

Around eleven, Sugimoto came by with two guys.

"Everything's been taken care of."

"Well done. Now we can relax a bit."

We managed to make the switch-over without anyone connected to the drug routes getting arrested. That was important. Police surveillance over a new route wasn't strict. They'd be under the impression that our gang wasn't involved with drugs—at least for a while.

"It's looking like Kawano will be handling drugs over at the main family."

"How long will it last?"

"Three months. Kawano will probably get caught. They probably won't get as far as indicting Brother Kurauchi. They got the routes back, but they'll get caught before they make any money."

"Don't let things slide, Sugimoto. You've got to keep a close watch on the younger ones, especially at a time like this."

"Yes, I know."

"Well, why don't you enjoy yourself tonight, have a drink?"

Sugimoto nodded.

I sat at the counter and called only Ayumi over. I'd only make the younger guys nervous if I hung out with them.

I listened to news about the club. The bartender Fujii made sure my glass was always filled, but he didn't try to interrupt our conversation. From afar, it probably looked as though Ayumi and I were getting intimate.

"So what should we do about Emi?"

"Don't put her to work just yet. She earned us a lot of money. Why don't you give her paid leave for a month?"

"You're changing, dear."

"Yeah, you too."

"For the worse, I guess. But if it means getting to run a place like this, I don't think I mind having changed for the worse."

When I'd been at the Boss's beck and call, I was full of discontent. I needed to curse him out in private, and acquired the habit of talking to myself.

That said, I wondered if I was truly content now. I'd spent so much of my life being dissatisfied that I didn't really know what it meant not to feel that way.

I finished off my drink and Fujii, standing nearby, gave Ayumi a questioning look. Ayumi nodded. Fujii got me another whiskey.

"Do you have any gripes?"

"Nope, nothing. You've been kind enough to give me a job while my son's locked up."

"No, I didn't mean it that way. More like...they're making the tonic water sweeter these days. You know, stuff like that."

"I try not to let those things bother me. Once you start thinking like that, there's no end to it."

"That's true." I sipped at my whiskey. At the very least, I had no complaints about how Fujii made his drinks. There was a hearty burst of laughter at the booth where my guys were.

**5**

It was past one by the time I got in a cab.

The cab dropped Ayumi off at the apartment in Shibuya. She probably figured that I wouldn't be of any use to her being as drunk as I was.

"Sugi-chan keeps telling me not to let you go around by yourself at night."

"It's okay. I'm going home and getting into bed."

"I don't understand why you don't just crash at my place. You're so stubborn about the dumbest things."

I told the cabbie to drive on.

He drove for a while before I told him to go to Nakameguro. At this hour, it only took about five minutes.

I got off a little ways before we reached Yoshie's apartment, and walked along the river.

"Just as I'd planned," I was muttering again. "Smooth and easy." But that was all I said. Probably because I wasn't dissatisfied. With me, talking to myself meant wishing misfortune on somebody, usually. Either that or just a string of foul words.

"I hope you die. Soon." I was thinking of the Boss lying asleep in the hospital. But that was all I could come up with. My feelings towards him had changed a little since the days when he treated me like a servant.

I lit a cigarette and smoked it as I walked. What if someone made an attempt on my life right now? It crossed my mind for just a second. I probably wouldn't be able to get away. There was no guarantee I wouldn't be attacked.

"If you're going to die, you're going to die."

After I muttered those words, a feeling, something like

fear, suddenly engulfed me. I felt confused. I'd never expe-
rienced anything like it before. Before I realized it, I had
started walking more quickly.

"What the hell's wrong with me?"

I tried to shake off the feeling that was starting to cling
to me. But the more I tried, the more it clung.

I reached Yoshie's apartment in a state of relief.

I took the elevator up to the sixth floor.

I pressed her doorbell. After the second ring, I saw the
shadow of a figure coming toward the door. I stood where
she could see me clearly through the fish-eye lens. I heard
her unlock the door.

"It's kind of late."

"Bad time?"

"No, just unusual." Yoshie was wrapped in a pink
bathrobe and was without a trace of make-up.

I sat down in the dining area, taking off my jacket.
Yoshie took it and put it on a hanger.

"Would you like a drink? Or...?"

"I want a bath. I'm beat."

"This is unusual. You used to say you couldn't relax in a
bath unless it was at your place. It'll take about ten minutes."

I nodded. No matter how you looked at her, Yoshie was
a well-bred, mature woman. To look at her, you'd never
think she had a not-so-secret desire to make other women
miserable.

"I bought you some new underwear."

"Yeah, okay."

The sliding door in the back room was shut. Her place was a one-bedroom, and it was Western-style.

"She's still here."

"Who?"

"Her."

"Yoko?"

I'd brought her here three days ago. I lent her to Yoshie. I thought maybe we'd put her body to work. I gave Yoshie some dope, just in case she could use them on her.

But if Yoko put up a fuss, Yoshie probably couldn't have shot her up. She wouldn't have been able to stop her, either, if she'd wanted to go home.

I could have simply beaten up the girl, but I also wanted to see Yoshie at her best.

"What do you mean, she's still here?"

"I'm being very careful with her." She laughed, and I saw her false teeth. Too white.

I got up and opened the sliding door at the back.

Yoko's naked body was lying on the carpet. She was asleep. Her hair was tangled, she looked thinner, and her eyelids were twitching as if she had some nervous tic. But she wasn't tied up or anything. She had a lot of marks on her arm from the shots.

"Looks like she let you shoot her up all nice and quiet." Nothing about the scene moved me, seeing her like that.

"It was easy. She was already pretty drunk by the time you brought her over here. I just gave her some more to drink."

"Didn't it bother her, the drugs plus the booze?"

"I didn't give her any while she was still drunk. I just made her feel real good." Yoshie's tone became glib.

"What do you mean, made her feel good?"

"I made her happy. I took her to places I don't go with you."

I didn't catch on right away.

"There are some things a woman can do better than a man, you know. And that's what drove this one crazy. First while she was drunk, and then when she was sober, and then when she was high. From now on, I won't even have to touch her for her to crave the drugs."

"How do you do it?"

"That's a secret. Anyway, it wouldn't do any good for a man to know."

"It doesn't work between a man and a woman?"

"Something like that. I don't really like it myself. And I hated the person who did it to me."

"Yoko'll hate you, too."

"I've been so careful with her, she'll go through hell but not resent me at all. She'll crawl around in that hell for, say, three or four years, and come out an empty shell. She'll delight me all along the way. You can bring more of them here. All the more welcome if they're girls that you've got a thing for."

"Women can be damn scary, too."

"That's right. Men only kill each other. Women can

inflict hell on each other. This one'll make money. In another year, she'll have the kind of body that'll drive men crazy. I'll keep tabs on how much drugs she gets. I'll give her as much as she wants when she's made a man happy. In time, her body'll only be there to make men happy. And then you should try her out one more time."

"You're fucking amazing."

"If you really think so, you'll bring me another one like her. As long as you like the girl. And if you *really* like her, that's even better. Or will it break your heart?"

"I'm *yakuza*, you know." I crouched down and touched Yoko's body. I didn't try to wake her up. I wondered if Yoko still thought that I wasn't *yakuza*, but some manager at an electrical company.

"I'm getting in the tub."

"Okay." Yoshie sounded more lady-like again.

Yoshie began unbuttoning my shirt. She took off my belt and pants. I stood there until she took my underwear off, too. She touched my scar with her fingertips. She kept touching me in that gentle way for a while.

"Fuck me while that girl's watching."

"Sounds good."

"I know I don't have such a great body. But I can be of use to you."

"I like that." I went in the bathroom.

I eased into the water. I didn't feel it sting the scar on my body. I didn't have any scars on my heart anyway.

"I'm *yakuza*," I muttered, sitting in the tub. I muttered

the word again, soaking in the water. It didn't seem as though I was ever going to break this habit.

# LIKE A DOG

## 1

Four young guys were standing around in the hospital lobby. One of them noticed me and came running over to the elevator to press the button.

"Sano Uncle is just—"

"Don't stand around looking so obvious. Stay in the corner or something and don't get in the way of civilians."

He lowered his head. It wasn't that I cared what civilians thought about us *yakuza*. I just didn't want to attract the cops' attention. Nothing more.

He held down the elevator button, keeping the doors open. None of the other people in the lobby got on with us. They didn't even look like they would.

"Two men should be enough for the lobby. A hospital lobby is public space. What was Kurauchi-san thinking? He's the one who'll get in trouble if the cops start nosing around," Sugimoto spat out as the doors slid shut.

The drug routes we'd returned—fully aware of what would happen—were indeed crushed by the cops in less than three months' time. And to compensate for the shortage created by the loss of those routes, traffic on ours increased.

The elevator was unbelievably slow. It took so long before the doors slid open to the sixth floor that I had plenty of time to think about what I should say when I saw Kurauchi.

There were two guys here too, in the hallway on the sixth floor.

The Boss was in a special room. He'd been in there for more than half a year, and that alone must have cost Kurauchi a pretty penny. As for me, I just brought him a get-well gift of two hundred thousand in cash on my monthly visits.

"I wonder if this is it, finally." The words that came out of my mouth when I greeted Kurauchi, who came out of the hospital room, were not the ones I'd considered in the elevator.

"There's no specific problem in his case—it's more like his whole body's breaking down. He's not suffering. He's been lying in that bed for months."

"And now?"

"He's sleeping. I think the medicine kicked in. I was watching him…and he looked so helpless lying there. I'd feel much better if he gave some sign, any sign, even if it's to say he's in pain."

"You better prepare yourself for the worst, Kurauchi-san."

The doctor had said to summon his close relations. In other words, the doctor's verdict was in: the end was near.

Kurauchi looked tired. His cheeks were hollow and he had dark circles under his eyes. We'd only heard about the Boss's condition last night, so his haggard look couldn't have been from worrying about the Old Man.

He'd been having it out with the cops. Kurauchi'd tried all of a sudden to double the shaky drug routes I'd given back. He'd neglected to be patient and didn't close up all of the gaps beforehand. Maybe he didn't know better. All Kurauchi had done until recently was work under the Boss, as his financial advisor.

Five of his young guys had been arrested. The drug routes had been crushed, and if he made any false moves, things could turn and bite him in his very own ass, too.

Serving your time. He hadn't really served his. He'd only been behind bars once—when he was younger, for blackmail. Once a *yakuza* had served time, he could sniff out the different types of handcuffs.

"Can we see him?"

"For a little while."

"Let's go see the Boss, Kurauchi-san. Burn his living image into our brains."

"Yeah." Kurauchi called over a nurse and whispered something in her ear.

The Boss was all tangled up in cords, and had tubes coming out of his nose. There were several different machines near his bed. It didn't seem at all like a hospital.

More like some odd and unfamiliar place. Was this what it meant to be on your deathbed?

"What's all this? We can't even talk to the Boss?"

"That's impossible, Tanaka Brother. The Boss hasn't spoken a word in several months."

When your time was about to run out, you regained consciousness for a moment. That's what I thought. For a minute only, or perhaps a mere second, you came back to the world. You died knowing exactly what you were doing: dying.

"So this is the so-called 'critical condition'? You don't know when he's going to die? That's not fair!"

"It can't be helped," Kurauchi said. "It's the center of his brain that's damaged."

"He'll wake up when he's about to die. He'll definitely wake up. Otherwise, how's he supposed to die?"

"We all want him to wake up."

"He'll wake up. I'll wait here until he does." There were lots of things I wanted to ask him when he woke up. More than I could reasonably ask. Why didn't he appoint me successor? Why did he suddenly lose the desire to expand his gang, relying instead on what he could milk from others? Why did he make me handle all the dangerous work? Did he really not care for me?

"Brother."

"I'm not moving from here, Kurauchi-san."

"Please be reasonable."

"Someone has to be around to tell him he's going to

die."

"You can't do that, Tanaka Brother. He can't talk, he can't even hear."

You dotard! That was the first thing I wanted to tell him. Hey, Boss, people from Hell are here to pick you up! It was my task to tell him that.

For just a moment, his face blurred before me. I realized that I was holding his hand and crying. I couldn't believe myself. His hand was tiny and wrinkled, cold. Like a monkey's hand. I couldn't let go of it.

"Tanaka?"

"Uncles."

It was Ohyama and Sano. The touch of Sano's hand on my shoulder was full of compassion.

"There's no use. No use. Brother managed to live this long and now he can die in a hospital bed. Maybe it's better this way."

Ohyama's voice resonated with reassurance. I still couldn't let go of the Boss's hand. He hit me with that hand. He'd milked me dry. And maybe did with it something else I never even realized.

"Hey, Tanaka. That should do." I could feel gentle pressure from Sano's hand.

I let go of the Boss and wiped my tears with the palm of my hand. I realized that I'd been crouching down.

"Is it really the end for the Boss, Kurauchi-san?"

"That's what the doctor's saying. His body's not responding, and he might go at anytime. This morning or even right now."

"I see."

"Apparently, if he's hooked up to the machines, he'll last another three or four days. But I don't think even Shinichi-san's thinking of taking things that far."

Shinichi was the Boss's real son. He had nothing to do with the *yakuza* world and was making an honest living. The Boss even had two grandchildren, but I'd heard that Shinichi wasn't too excited about his father adoring and doting on them.

I went out into the hallway and found Sugimoto waiting for me.

"It's not exactly the best time to discuss funeral arrangements, but…" As the oldest member of the Clan, Ohyama spoke up. The main family would handle all the arrangements. There would be a huge amount of condolence money coming in from all the other gangs they had relations with, and all of it would go to the main family. Kurauchi would continue to lead it, of course.

"I don't have any complaints. It would be unheard of for the duty to fall on anyone else." It seemed Kurauchi had started turning to Ohyama for help. Sano had divided up his gang, and others had been arrested, so now the main family counted only about twenty. My gang, numbering over thirty, had become larger.

"Tanaka, I'm glad I ran into you here. I'll let Mizuta know what's up."

"Uncle Ohyama, who cares what a punk like me thinks

and does? What matters is, where do you stand?"

"I'll be Kurauchi's guardian. Sano divided up the gang, so there's no one else who can do it."

Kurauchi had probably asked him. He'd probably realized by now that the drug routes I'd returned had been full of holes, and was bitter about having been cheated. Even then, had he worked things right, the drug routes wouldn't have gone under. There was no use in his moping about it to anyone.

I wasn't particularly threatened by Kurauchi and Ohyama teaming up. I knew from watching Ohyama's moves during the war that he wasn't the type to get seriously involved in anything that didn't directly involve his gang.

"So is it really the end for the Clan Boss?" Sugimoto asked when we were in the car. Yoshino was driving. It was the same old domestic car. Once the Boss's funeral was over, I wouldn't object to a Mercedes. Our branch could easily spare that kind of money.

"Everyone thinks it must've been a big shock for you, Boss. All the juniors at the main family are saying they'd have preferred you to be the successor."

"It's probably the end, for the main family. Once the pieces come falling, it all comes down pretty fast."

"It's about power, isn't it—with *yakuza*?"

No matter which point of view you took, we were on the rise. And not much time had passed since I'd been forced to branch out. Even the Uncles had to mind what I thought.

The city was passing me by outside the window. I stared at it vacantly, thinking about the Boss. Why had I cried? I'd wanted to curse him.

I'd spent over twenty years under him. I'd taken it for granted that he'd always be around to hold me back, keep me down. I had never seriously thought about what it'd be like once he was gone.

"What's wrong, Boss?" Sugimoto was peering into my face.

"I'm going over to Ayumi's. We're not going to do anything over the top, got it? Just be patient."

"I got you. The cops can give us trouble in times like these. I'll call Sister and explain the whole situation about the Clan Boss."

"Thanks."

Ayumi's place in Shibuya was conveniently located as far as getting over to the hospital was concerned.

I turned my gaze out the window again, to the passing city.

## 2

There was something innocent and childlike about Ayumi when she wasn't wearing any make-up. But I noticed wrinkles around the corners of her eyes that hadn't been there several years ago.

I sipped at the coffee she'd made, staring out the window down at the street. It wasn't a main road and there were more parked cars than moving ones. It was still morning.

Business was good over at the Akasaka club. It was because she'd gotten together a good bunch of girls. Customers still came by asking for Ayumi as well. There'd been three instances of trouble with customer accounts up to now, and I'd gotten involved, bringing in twelve million. There still weren't any rumors about *yakuza* backing. There were a lot of ways I could get involved so they'd think they were in trouble with the debt collector rather than with the club directly.

"You don't seem like you're willing to settle down and move in here anytime soon." Ayumi had thrown a gown over her negligee and was removing her nail polish. "I mean, I understand that you like living on your own and all."

"Then shut up about it."

"You only have one way of seeing a relationship between a man and a woman, don't you." Ayumi was grouchy in the morning. She had low blood pressure. These days she'd been complaining about her liver too. If I started any trouble with her when she was like this, it always ended in disaster.

"He meant more to me than my real parents. A lot's happened over the years, but he's been like a father to me for more than twenty of them."

"There isn't much you can do. No one lives forever." Ayumi was sitting on the sofa, looking as though she was ready to fall asleep again. "Now they call you Boss."

"Not in the way I hoped for once."

"Anyway, it's not about outdoing the main family. Sugi-chan was saying that at the club. Who cares how it all came about anyway?"

"Maybe the Boss was planning to be around a little longer. Maybe it was just easier for him to have me do the dirty work. If you think about it, I was lucky."

"You never know when your luck's going to change and things start going your way. There were times when I cried myself to sleep, thinking what a horrible man you were. It's true. And to think I'm living like this now!"

I finished my coffee and went over to the pot to pour myself another cup.

I didn't think I'd given her such a great life. I was giving her the kind of life that offset my own lifestyle. That's what it came down to. If I became more powerful, Ayumi would get another club like the one she had in Akasaka. Two would become three, and three eventually four.

I sat down next to Ayumi, taking out a cigarette. Ayumi got the Dupont.

I wondered why I'd cried. I'd clutched the Boss's hand and cried. I couldn't stop thinking about it. Was it simply because I felt so close to him that I hated him and wished he'd croak?

He'd never done anything for me. Other than giving me a chance to live as a *yakuza* from age nineteen to forty-three.

"Sugi-chan said that you're beginning to seem more and more like a father for the guys. He says the other gangs are recognizing your status. And it's good that you didn't go for the Mercedes as soon as you got your gang together."

I wasn't really interested in fast cars, fancy clothes, or expensive apartments. Ambition. I'd wanted to rise up in the *yakuza* world. That was the only thing on my mind for twenty years.

It could have been that the Boss had been a little afraid of me. That was what I started suspecting after he got sick. He must have been able to relax a bit more around someone like Kurauchi, who only thought about money. Maybe he could foresee how things would turn out if Kurauchi became his successor. But there was no denying that he didn't give a damn about what would happen to the Clan once he was gone. I was the same way.

"I won't ask you to register your name with mine, though."

"Quit it."

I just couldn't live with her. I'd lived alone my whole life.

"Always the same thing."

"Quit it," I said.

Ayumi was quiet. She must have been thinking of the time I messed her up so bad that she couldn't go out for almost two weeks. The best way to shut a woman up was to thrash her face.

It was better not to start a family if you were *yakuza*. That used to be my philosophy. A *yakuza* didn't have the right to taste ordinary pleasures. I didn't mean that self-deprecatingly. I believed that if you lived an ordinary life, you lost your capacity for extraordinary things. I'd seen it happen to so many.

The Boss, for example. Things could have been different if he'd just held out, but inevitably he caved. After he had grandchildren, his main concern was protecting them. Even then, he had to have two young chippies on the side.

Ayumi stretched. Apparently, she was now ready to start her day. It was all she could do just to get me a cup of coffee when I'd first arrived.

"Do you need to let Sugi-chan know that you're here?"

Apparently her mind had started working, too. A cigarette between her lips, she went to pour herself a cup of coffee. I never got coffee for Ayumi.

"So you're forty-three. That's a good age," Ayumi said unexpectedly, sipping her coffee.

When I was in my twenties, I used to dislike imagining what it'd be like to be forty. Crotchety old *yakuza*. That was what I used to think when I saw *yakuza* in their forties.

Now any guy under thirty seemed like a kid to me. It was all a matter of perspective, people's ages. There was no denying that my body just wasn't what it used to be. But I felt I could push myself if I wanted to. It wasn't as if I'd be playing rugby. Ten seconds was all you needed to kill someone.

Ayumi went into the bedroom and changed into a blouse and skirt. She had run a brush through her hair and had put on a little make-up, too.

"Should I make you something? It's almost noon."

I nodded, looking through the paper. There was a war going on between the gangs in the Kansai region. These days everyone had guns. Back when I was in my early twenties, the saying was that one gun was worth fifty troops. But nowadays, shoot-outs between young guys weren't unusual.

The gangs in the paper didn't have much to do with me. The Boss's gang was part of a national syndicate designated by the police as *yakuza*, and he paid them certain membership dues. My gang was part of that group, too, but I paid only the main family.

Whoever stood at the top must have come into a lot of money without having to do much. I'd never even thought about it before.

"Spaghetti all right?"

"You don't have any soba or udon noodles?"

"If I'd known you were coming, I'd have bought some."

"Yeah, whatever's fine."

I folded up the paper. You were supposed to conduct a war so that neither the cops nor the papers got wind of it. Otherwise you'd end up sending a bunch of guys to prison.

It ended up costing a lot. The trick was to dispatch a hit man when things were winding down. That way you'd only have to send one guy to jail.

I turned on the TV.

I couldn't relax. My whole body jolted when the phone rang. It was one of the girls from Ayumi's club.

The TV show was broadcasting live from some amusement park. Something about a new roller coaster. Two girls were on the ride. It started moving. Their car went zooming and spiraling upside-down along the rails. The girls got off. "We couldn't even scream," they said when a mike was thrust in front of them.

"What the hell's the big deal?" I muttered, changing the channel. Comedy, variety, news. I couldn't find anything worth watching on any channel.

Something smelled good. I remembered I hadn't had breakfast. Ayumi was a good cook. She used to prepare all the food herself when she ran the other bar.

I flipped off the TV and stared out the window, smoking. It was a clear day. We were on the twelfth floor, so I could see pretty far off into the distance. My place in Kitasuna couldn't compare to this. I bought this place partly for the sake of the junior members. Sometimes I brought them over here. They called Ayumi "Sister," and she didn't seem to mind.

Ayumi called. Lunch was ready. Spaghetti and salad.

"Do you want beer?"

"Just water."

"That's strange."

"What, I'm supposed to be drinking beer while the Boss is dying?"

"I thought it might take your mind off things."

I didn't badmouth the Boss in front of anyone. I was so careful to curse him only in private that I acquired the habit of talking to myself. Ayumi probably thought I was really worried about the Boss.

Maybe I was. I'd never even imagined that I'd cry, but as soon as I saw him, the tears wouldn't stop. I guess somewhere deep down, even as I cursed him, I must have felt that the Boss *was* my Old Man.

I wound the spaghetti around my fork. I pushed it into my mouth. I'd never really been particular about what I ate. It wouldn't be inaccurate to say that I ate so I wouldn't starve to death.

"The president of N. Corporation comes to our club pretty often."

"Oh yeah? Who for?"

"Me."

"Good. That's good."

"Are you sure putting me to work in that way is a good idea?"

"Don't worry. Yours isn't the only club we run. It's bound to happen soon. Once you get hold of a big one, you can start over at another place."

"So you'll open up another place?"

"I'm thinking of making it three. The only problem is

where. There're only so many places in Tokyo where we have the clout to set up shop."

"Why don't you just pay the other gangs compensation, like we do with our club?"

"How long do you think a *yakuza* can go on paying up to another gang? Eventually I want to work things out so I don't even have to pay for that place either."

"I don't want any fighting at our club."

"Why would I risk having my own property smashed up? I can handle it. I've got something in mind."

"Well, that's okay then."

Ayumi put a forkful of spaghetti in her mouth. I didn't really like seeing women eat. I did my best not to watch. Somehow I could tolerate it with Ayumi though.

I ate a little and then doused my spaghetti in tabasco sauce. It tasted fine the way it was. I just wanted something stronger. The only thing at hand was tabasco.

I sat down on the sofa when I'd finished eating and went back to the paper.

"I bought two kimonos."

"Yeah?"

"You never have anything to say about that sort of thing."

"Women look best naked."

"Oh please."

Guys in my world liked to dress up their women. That kind of guy did his best to make himself look good too. I didn't give a damn.

I read the paper all the way through from front to back. It must have been the first time in all my forty-three years.

"I'm off."

I did up my necktie. I always wore a gray suit, but I'd probably have to wear black for the Boss's funeral. I could probably go like this to the wake. It'd seem too much like I'd been waiting for him to die if I wore black.

"What if Sugi-chan calls?"

"I'm going out. Sugimoto won't call here."

I left the apartment. I walked for a while. I'd said I was going out, but I hadn't really decided where.

Maybe I'd go over to Nakameguro, I thought suddenly. Once it occurred to me, I didn't have to think twice. I called Yoshie from a telephone booth—and Sugimoto too while I was at it.

No news yet from the hospital.

## 3

I took a bath as soon as I got to Yoshie's.

I lay down on the bed, with just a towel around my waist. A little while later, Yoshie came and lay down next to me after her shower. She touched my scar with her fingertips. It hadn't been ministered to by a doctor, so it was incredibly ugly, jagged almost.

"So tell me about the time you got this."

It was always the same. I told her a somewhat exaggerated version of how I got the scar on my shoulder. Like how much blood I'd lost, what it felt like when I got hurt. Those were the things I exaggerated, and it excited Yoshie.

I wanted to have sex with Yoshie, not Ayumi. I didn't know why. I just felt like it. Stories of injuries and blood. Of murder. That kind of stuff was all foreplay for this woman. She wasn't exceptionally beautiful. Just your average woman, and usually quite modest.

"I don't really remember what it was like when I got stabbed. Things were so intense. All you can really feel is the heat. Then you're shoving the guy off you and you touch it. It's hot. Not wet. Sticky. That's how blood gets after a while."

Yoshie put her lips to my wound. From time to time she let out a low moan.

"And you're desperate when you're sewing it up, too. Your fingers are all bloody, and you're trying to close it up one stitch at a time. You don't even notice how much it hurts. Gotta hurry and sew it up, stop the blood from flowing. And the needle's all slippery from the blood."

Yoshie let out another low moan.

"The worst is when you pull out the needle. When you think you've managed to close it up, you pull it out really hard. There aren't any words to describe the feeling of thread passing through flesh."

Yoshie was trembling, fixated on my wound. I was telling the story with more intensity than usual.

When we finished, both Yoshie and I were breathing hard. I didn't consider her strange. In fact, she was a lot like me.

"Let's stay like this a little longer."

Unusual for Yoshie. I lay still while she caressed my wound.

The phone rang.

I jumped off the bed before Yoshie could get up. I gestured for her to hurry up and answer it.

She started chatting and laughing on the phone. I lost interest in the call. I lit a cigarette and lay down on the bed.

It was probably a customer. Yoshie had eleven girls working for her now, and I was getting quite a bit of cash out of it. Eight of the eleven had favored customer status with me. Most of the money they earned selling their bodies went straight into my drugs. I sold them the drugs straight from my routes, at a discount.

All eleven girls were pretty much amateurs. Yoko was the only girl who'd worked at a bar, but I was the one who had brought her in. The other ten Yoshie found on her own. They were bank tellers, shop girls, and housewives. Yoshie had a strange gift.

"The Boss is about to die, you know."

"Aren't you the Boss?"

"No, my Boss. We're a branch family. I'm talking about the Clan Boss."

"Oh."

Yoshie had never shown any interest in the *yakuza*

world. Her only concern was interference with her business. I acted as Yoshie's shield, as a kind of buffer.

"I'm going to stick around here for a while. I have to let them know where they can reach me."

I realized we were both naked. Yoshie's eyes gave off a strange glint. She wanted to go at it again. I knew that look all too well. Sex while waiting for a man to die. That excited Yoshie.

I was assaulted by a curious mixture of fatigue and excitement. I didn't move away when Yoshie leaned over me.

"That was amazing," Yoshie said when we'd finished. "Why can't someone be dying all the time?"

Naked, I put a cigarette in my mouth and stretched out on the bed. I blew out a cloud of smoke.

Yoshie was lying next to me, occasionally letting out a deep sigh. It wasn't as though she always jumped on me every time I dropped in. More like one time out of every three. Whether or not she was depraved, I didn't really know. I just knew she couldn't be normal.

I felt as if time were crawling by. 3:00 p.m. finally rolled around.

I'd finished my cigarette but Yoshie still didn't budge. I didn't really feel like moving either.

"Everything okay?" I said, staring at the ceiling. What I meant was whether the cops had an eye on the business. Perhaps she was having problems with other gangs. So far there hadn't been a single incident, even though she was conducting an illegal business. The eleven girls were behaving.

"As long as you keep the medicine coming my way."

"That's no problem."

"If I had more customers, I'd place more girls under my control."

She had about thirty clients. Seemed her regulars brought plenty of other potential clients, but the numbers she pulled from them weren't that high. Yoshie had her standards.

"I thought this kind of business was outdated," I admitted, "but when I see you at work, it's obviously more efficient than running a Soapland brothel."

"You can't suck them dry if they're working at a Soapland. Girls can earn money really fast in those places."

I never asked Yoshie why it was that she put so much passion into ruining women. When she talked about the women she'd sucked the life out of, she didn't reveal the slightest emotion.

"I think we better watch it with Yoko, though," Yoshie said.

"Why?"

"Well, before she started crawling around in her private hell, there was a guy."

"And she still let me have her?"

"Yoko didn't love him. But he really loved her. Still does, apparently. He's been sniffing around for her, and he's finally traced her to my place."

"You mean he wants to rescue her?"

"Not that he could. He only found my place because Yoko came running here to get away from him."

I had no idea what she'd done to Yoko. She'd definitely been shot up with a ton of drugs, because I'd supplied them, but it couldn't have been the drugs alone.

"Tanaka-san. Better be careful with some of those young men." Yoshie finally moved and lit up a cigarette. "He did everything to find her, and he got her to tell him about you."

"You saying a civilian can take me on?"

"I don't know, but it's entirely possible that he'll do something unimaginable."

"I have a pretty good imagination. You don't think he'll run to the cops?"

"Even if he does, she's got nothing to do with you now, and if they come here, I'm more like her big sister than anything else."

"You assign clients to certain girls."

"They can't prove it. And as far as Yoko's concerned, I'm being extra careful with her. It's not like I brought her over here myself."

I didn't ask her what she meant by "extra careful." Yoshie didn't seem to appreciate my prying into her methods.

"Well, I'll be careful then."

"I'll be done with Yoko soon. I give her three more months."

"That's all it takes, huh?"

"Well, she's an exception."

The girl I'd fallen for. That's what I said when I handed her over to Yoshie. Something about that must have excited Yoshie. That's why she was ruining Yoko more quickly than the others.

I got up and went in the shower. I'd fallen for a girl that still reeked of pee, a girl who worked at a regular Shinjuku bar. It felt like such a long time ago.

After my shower, I changed into the new underwear laid out for me. Yoshie did stuff like that without saying anything about it. I let her do as she pleased. I thought it best not to get involved with certain things. Some things were done my way, others she did her way.

"Would you like something to eat?" Yoshie had reverted back to her usual well-mannered self.

"I don't really know what's going to happen now. Get me some sushi for tonight."

"With beer, then."

Yoshie had cooked for me once, and once was enough. If I of all people felt that way, her cooking skills must have been abnormally bad.

I called the office.

"Boss, I'm on pins and needles myself, waiting."

"I guess the Boss's heart was in excellent condition."

"Generally, when they call the patient's relatives, it means the end."

"There are some things the doctor can't predict,

Sugimoto."

"In any case, things are going fine with the gang. I've got a few guys stationed, though."

"Fine."

"Should I send someone over there as protection?"

"What the hell for?"

"Times like this, I don't think we should be taking any chances."

"Thanks for your concern, Sugimoto. Times like this, you've got to have tight control over the territory, make sure no one tries to move in, take advantage."

"Okay."

As I hung up the phone, I wondered if the Boss was still wheezing like that in the hospital. I no longer felt weepy over his death. Rather, I felt like patting him on the back for his inconsiderate tenacity. Way to go, Old Man.

It was still light outside.

Kurauchi was going to take over as successor the moment the Boss died. Rebuilding the enfeebled main family was probably beyond Kurauchi. Disbanding was a distinct possibility. The Uncles would probably do their best to keep that from happening. Perhaps I'd be asked to take care of some main family members and be designated Kurauchi's successor.

The pressing question until then was how to weaken Kurauchi.

The main family was already quite weak, but I needed to reduce it further to a small gang, say of five or six.

All I needed was another war. Kurauchi's cowardice was bound to be his downfall. Even if there were untapped resources in him, there was no way he'd survive a full-blown conflict.

Yoshie brought me a glass of beer. I downed it in one gulp.

Maybe it was a good thing that I'd been made to branch out. If I'd become the successor, there would have been enough trouble to bring me down. I had built up my gang with my own two hands. Since Kurauchi was pathetic, it wasn't all that difficult for me. If the Boss had lived longer and had had his eyes on me, things would've been much tougher for me.

In other words, I was lucky. That's probably what it was. It was probably the first time in my *yakuza* life that I'd thought of myself as a lucky man.

I drank two beers, staring out the window. I still only had the towel around my waist. Yoshie put on some music. I'd never been interested in music, really. I never had much music in my life, including as a kid. As far as I knew, Yoshie's hobby was music. She had a whole wall lined with records and CDs.

I poured myself a third beer, and watched the foam disappear. That alone took up quite a bit of time. When I was on the inside, I did what I could, trying to think of something that would help pass the time. I had a sickening amount of time, and I killed it joylessly. I'd no choice but to tell myself that I was doing it all for the Boss.

"You have all kinds of strange habits." Yoshie came over to me, holding a glass. "The longer you stick around, the more I find out about you."

"Like what?"

"Like you always pour your beer with your left hand. And you don't drink it all right away. You take a small sip, like you're making sure it hasn't been poisoned. And every five minutes, you touch the tip of your nose with your finger. And when you light a cigarette, you squint your left eye."

"That's enough."

"Are you mad?"

"No. I know some of your habits too now. But I just don't say."

"Good. You shouldn't."

I didn't even feel like asking her why. I was tired. I was getting bored of sitting around waiting. There was nothing I could do about it. There was no point in getting irritated. It was like being behind bars.

**4**

It was after 10:00 p.m. by the time I heard from Sugimoto.

I put on a tie and rushed out of Yoshie's apartment, jacket in hand.

It took fifteen minutes to get to the hospital.

A bunch of main family people were hanging around in the hospital lobby. One of them rushed over to me as I hurried over to the elevator.

The Boss was in the basement mortuary.

Kurauchi got up from his chair as I entered.

I lifted the white sheet that was covering the Old Man's face. He looked strangely calm. His eyes were closed, and he looked as if he were sleeping.

"He didn't suffer any. Apparently it was like he went into a deep sleep."

"Well that's not a bad way to go for a *yakuza*. Eh, Kurauchi-san?"

"Yes, that's true."

"The Boss always used to say that it wouldn't be strange for a *yakuza* to die in the gutter somewhere. And look at him, dying in a proper hospital." I'd started crying again. This time I was well aware of it. Kurauchi was crying too. The moment I saw him like that, just for that moment, I felt close to him like he was family.

I sat down next to Kurauchi.

Sugimoto came in and clasped the Boss's hand in his own. All the Uncles came too. It hit me again that the Old Man was really dead. Part of me couldn't believe he was dead, even though his body was laid out right there, in front of me.

"Is everything ready, Kurauchi?" someone asked, and we both looked up.

"I've let all those nearby know, and the rest I'll inform

tomorrow morning. We'll have the wake tomorrow and the funeral the day after."

"Sounds good. You can use any of our guys." It was Ohyama. Actually brought several with him. If only he'd volunteered as many during the war, I thought to myself.

The arriving car wasn't a hearse but a station wagon. The Uncles, Kurauchi, and I put the Boss in the back of the car.

It was night, and there wasn't much traffic.

Kurauchi's Mercedes was the lead car, then came the station wagon, followed by the Uncles' cars and finally mine.

"You keep wondering when, but when it actually happens, you can't believe it's real, you know," Sugimoto said, sitting next to me in the backseat. I'd brought seven other guys from my gang.

"No one made it in time."

Apparently they'd said that the Old Man would be okay until the following day, so even Kurauchi, whose turn it was on duty, left that evening. The Boss had died alone.

We arrived at Clan headquarters in thirty minutes. The main family members, whose numbers had fallen to under twenty, were all lined up, waiting for the Boss to arrive.

He was laid down on a futon put out in the back room. The people who'd come to see him reached a hundred, and the place was crowded like it hadn't been in a long time.

"Shinichi-san will be in charge of the services. The head of the funeral committee will be you, Uncle, and I'll take care of the rest," Kurauchi reported to Ohyama. It'd probably be best to leave the matter of condolence gifts to Kurauchi. That was the sort of thing he was good at.

In just under an hour, everyone inside had become calm and quiet.

"That'll do for tonight. I'll have our juniors make sure we don't run out of incense," Kurauchi said, coming into the room where the Uncles and I were sitting.

"Sounds good. Our presence will be a burden on the young men. Tanaka, let's get going for now."

I nodded and got up. It'd be best if the main family handled matters like incense.

I was seen to my car by a junior who belonged to the main family. I got in.

"Where to, Boss?"

"The office, Sugimoto. Everyone's there, right?"

"Every last one. Well, aside from the guys on the inside."

The question was whether or not they'd all rally at a time like this. There was a lot you could learn from that. There were guys you couldn't count on in a war, and this was a good time to find out who they were.

"We'll get the best flowers, and we'll have a million yen ready for the condolence gift," Sugimoto offered.

"Sounds about right."

My junior boss didn't say more. I remained silent, too, until we reached the office.

When we arrived at the office, the first thing I did was

to put on a black suit and tie. Then I called the juniors together and let them know the Boss had died. One of them was smoking, and Sugimoto knocked him over. The atmosphere in the office became tense.

I spoke for about fifteen minutes. It felt as if I'd never spoken at such length before. I couldn't believe how the words of praise kept coming out of my mouth, phrase after phrase. Some of the guys were nearly in tears.

When I'd finished, Sugimoto assigned everyone their duties for the next day and they were dismissed.

I sat at my desk in the back, and the guys bid me good night before they left.

We'd moved out of the cramped office into this more spacious one. Here I had my own room, and even if our gang expanded to a hundred members, in here there'd be enough room for all of us.

"So what are you going to do, Boss?" It was one of the young guys whose turn it was to stay the night. Usually there were two guys, but this evening there were four. The only other person left was Sugimoto.

"I'm staying here."

"But we don't have a futon."

"I wasn't planning on sleeping."

The junior nodded and bowed his head.

Sugimoto brought over two whiskey glasses. For a moment, I wondered if you were supposed to drink to a dead man alone. It depended on who it was. "Who" meaning, who was the deceased, and who you were drinking with.

"Old Parr, eh?" I said, glancing at the label.

Sugimoto poured out half a glass. There was no ice in the glass.

I downed the first glass in one swig. Sugimoto took small sips of his. One of the junior members thoughtfully brought over some ice and peanuts. My stomach was still burning.

"Tomorrow," Sugimoto said, "we've really got to move some of that dope along. The market's going dry because the main family's routes aren't supplying anything anymore."

"Four or five guys should be enough."

"Three'd be plenty."

"We'll leave one to man the phones."

The rest would all go to the temple where the wake and the funeral were going to be held. Wearing the armbands of my gang. Kurauchi was making the arrangements for the wake and funeral. I was taking the back seat, but you only had to count the numbers to see that my gang was on the rise.

Silently, I tilted my glass. Out of consideration, the young guys on night watch didn't even turn on the TV. I didn't know if there was anything on at this time. It was almost three in the morning. I thought that if I went to my room in the back, they'd at least be able to nap, but I didn't feel like getting up.

"Why don't you all have a drink too," I said, but no one

made a move. Only after Sugimoto nodded did one of the guys come over for the bottle. Sugimoto ran a tight ship.

Around dawn, one of the guys went over to a 24-hour grocery store and bought us something to eat. Maybe Sugimoto had instructed him; he'd also bought tooth-brushes and disposable razors.

It was already eight in the morning by the time I got around to eating. The other guys had finished their meals a while ago.

Then I shaved, brushed my teeth, and combed my hair. At eight-fifty an ink-black Mercedes pulled up next to the office.

"It's only for two days. I borrowed it from a realtor friend. Other gangs'll be around, and I thought it'd look better this way."

It was just as Sugimoto said. You never knew when or how *yakuza* were going to make their judgments. If we showed up in that beat-up domestic car, there was no way it would raise me in the estimation of others.

But still, I thought it was unnecessary. I was about to say so, but Sugimoto turned to me and nodded before I could.

I wasn't uncomfortable in that Mercedes. Following us was a line of six cars containing my men. A small parade. I'd probably end up having to buy a Mercedes. I might have to handle a risky job to pay for it.

We arrived at the temple.

The funeral worker was already setting up fresh flowers

at the Buddhist altar. Most of the members of the main family had arrived, but no one from other gangs had come yet.

They seemed awed, taking in my troops.

"They're at your disposal, Kurauchi-san. Not just the guys, but me too."

"Thank you, Tanaka Brother. We're fine for now, but when guests start arriving, we'll need help directing traffic and greeting them." Kurauchi's reply was impeccable, if a little distant.

All the guests would see that my branch had more vigor than the main family. The idea couldn't have made Kurauchi too happy. Sugimoto had our guys spread out. I went and sat down inside the tent. The flowers kept arriving. There were quite a few from famous gangs.

"The Boss was a well-known *yakuza*. You only have to look at the flowers to see that," I said.

"That's true. He was around for a good while."

"Kurauchi-san, you're the second boss of the clan he started. You gotta shape up. After all, you're in charge of my branch too, you know." I lit a cigarette. One guy was always supposed to offer a light to the other. I could barely bring myself to do it. Because it meant acknowledging my inferior standing.

By noon, we'd finished all the arrangements for the wake. The food and drinks were going to be set out in the reception hall for the guests.

Sugimoto called me in to lunch. He'd somehow

procured just the right number of lunches for our gang. He was like an almost too perfect wife.

Around three, all the Uncles came around. So did a unit of riot police; a hundred cops took up their stations.

The wake began.

I didn't have any of my men stand anywhere near the reception table, where the gifts were submitted. I didn't want people to say that we had mobilized to filch consolation gifts. I had the guys concentrate on the duties of welcoming and seeing the mourners off, and conducting traffic.

Several bosses from well-known Kanto area gangs came. Counting the proxies, more than a dozen men of boss status were present.

"Got your own gang now, huh?" several of them said to me.

The announcement of my starting a gang had been modest; the gift money had amounted to only two million. So this funeral turned out to be my real announcement.

The wake ended at 10:00 pm.

Once the preparations for the funeral the next day were settled, I called everyone together. Kurauchi asked us to stay, but we'd already gone ahead and gotten some drinks and snacks at our office.

"I made sure I met everyone, too. I introduced myself as the junior boss of the Tanaka gang, and it seemed to impress people," Sugimoto said. We were in the Mercedes. I nodded silently. "And you looked every bit the part, Boss. I felt pretty proud. You had so much more presence than Kurauchi."

Something was wrong. This wasn't the way I wanted to live, and it didn't sit well. I had lived like a dog. I had assumed I would die like a dog. But now the Mercedes, and all the children.

Success. Why not? If I'd remained with the main family, as successor, things wouldn't have been that different. I had probably simply advanced to an age in life when such things just came along your way.

Truth be told, I was probably more suited to a life of threatening people, of beating them up. I couldn't shake off the punk in me.

"There'll be more people at the funeral tomorrow, sir. You should act as dignified as you did this evening, Boss."

"Is the main family doing things right?"

"They're kind of lifeless. A little jittery. They're worried about Kurauchi-san getting arrested, you know, for the old routes. I bet a lot of their young ones are planning to depend on us if that happens."

"I don't think Kurauchi's going to get caught."

"True, it's been a while since the bust. But they're worried just the same. Kurauchi-san too, I think."

Sugimoto laughed, in a low voice.

## 5

I left the office sometime after midnight.

Our private continuation of the Boss's wake had seemed more like an unrelated banquet, with all the booze and food.

"I'll have someone drive you home," Sugimoto said, escorting me out. "Two of the guys can't drink, so it won't be a dangerous ride."

"Nah, I'll take a cab."

"Please forgive them. Most of them hardly knew the Clan Boss."

"I'm not pissed or anything. It's just that they won't be able to relax while I'm around. Let 'em kick back once in a while. If you keep them too straight all the time, they'll do something they shouldn't somewhere they shouldn't."

"You're right."

"I'll be in Nakameguro. Let's try to make it to the office by eight tomorrow morning."

"I'll hail you a cab."

We walked over to the main road.

"Boss, let's crush the main family."

"Not tonight, Sugimoto. Please."

"I'm saying it *because* it's the wake. With Kurauchi succeeding him, the Clan Boss's got to be turning over in his grave. That's what I think."

"Kurauchi will probably team up with Ohyama Uncle."

"They don't have much of a future either."

"True." I got out a cigarette and Sugimoto offered me a light.

"We can crush them all, Boss. We have the power. It's because you were so patient when we were building ourselves up."

"Crush them all, huh?"

"We're *yakuza*, after all."

Sugimoto was still useful to me right now. He was probably thinking the same thing about me.

"Nakameguro," Sugimoto said to the cabbie.

I got in, my cigarette still between my lips.

"I'm sorry, sir, but could you put that out?" the cabbie said, and Sugimoto stuck his head in again.

"You don't want to die, do you, Mr. Cabbie?"

"Huh? Die?"

"Our Boss put out his cigarette? Why don't you try saying that again?"

"Quit it, Sugimoto. He's a civilian."

"Okay, but if he says something he shouldn't, give him a thrashing. I'm taking down his number. I'll call the company and get them to pay five or six million. Either that or I'll have him drowned."

"That's enough."

"Nakameguro, got it?" The door shut. The car pulled out slowly. The driver was obviously frightened. I stared out the window, and the city flowed past. I lit up another cigarette, but the driver didn't say anything. He didn't even open the window.

"Excuse me," he said when we stopped at a light. "Where in Nakameguro...?"

"By the station'll do."

"Okay."

The car started moving again. I turned toward the window again.

Suddenly, I recalled the first time I'd killed a man. No idea why I remembered just then. When I stabbed him and twisted the knife, my palms felt the bounciness of his guts through the blade. For some reason, I couldn't remember anything about my second killing. I only had a vivid recollection of the first.

"This is the station."

The car had stopped. I handed him two one-thousand yen bills.

I walked down the road along the river. It was less a river than a canal. But it was still called a river. You couldn't tell at night, but in the afternoon, you could see that water actually flowed in it.

Yoshie's apartment. A light in the entryway. Suddenly someone leapt out at me.

"You're Tanaka, aren't you."

It had to be a hit man, I thought. And if he were, there was no guarantee that he was alone.

"Yeah, I'm Tanaka."

"Where'd you hide Yoko?"

"Yoko?"

"Don't pretend you don't know her!" He stuck out his

right hand. He had a knife. He didn't even know how to knife someone. He was holding it the wrong way.

"Yoko? You mean the whore?"

"It's your fault she's become a prostitute."

"My fault? You trying to be funny? She's doing it because she likes it."

"I'm gonna fucking kill you!" he shouted. He was young. About twenty.

I threw down the jacket I'd flung over my arm. That alone made him jump back two paces. He put a hand in his pocket.

"So you were waiting for me?"

"For Yoko."

"Of course. But you got me instead. How come you got a knife? Planning to stab Yoko?"

"I was going to use it to make her listen."

"Doesn't listen to you? You little piece of shit. Why would she? The woman you love is a whore. Just buy her, you don't need to be doing this. I bet you aren't man enough to buy the woman you love. That's what makes you a little piece of shit."

I knew it'd mean trouble if I took him too seriously. But I did anyway. When I flung down my jacket, I dropped something else too.

"Yoko isn't—"

"She's a filthy whore."

He let out a low groan. He lunged at me. I didn't move out of his way. I took the knife straight in the stomach. He merely tore at my stomach, rather than stab it. He'd been holding the knife the wrong way; it couldn't cut deep.

He flinched at the sight of blood spurting from my stomach. I touched the wound underneath my shirt. Blood all over my fingers. Somehow it made me want to laugh.

"Why don't you kill me?" I took a step towards him. I laughed. I knew what would happen. He'd retreat. I took another step in.

"If you don't kill me, you're going to get killed yourself." Another step. He opened his mouth. He was shaking. I could see that plain and clear in the light of the street lamp. He was about to fall on his ass, and I kicked him in the chin. His back hit the railing and he sank down to the ground. He was going to piss in his pants.

With that, I took hold of myself again.

I looked down at him. His mouth was hanging open. He kept trembling and shaking. He couldn't speak.

I looked behind me, and picked my jacket up off the roadside.

I went back to the apartment and got in the elevator. Blood had seeped through my shirt, but it wasn't dripping.

Sixth floor. I rang the doorbell. Yoshie opened the door.

"Give me a thread and needle." I went straight into the bathroom and took off my clothes. My shirt was so soaked with blood that you could wring it out. There was a lot of blood on my pants too.

The gash was about ten centimeters long. But the knife had only gone in as far as three.

Yoshie brought me a needle and thread.

I stuck the needle through the skin on my side. It went in easily. I started sewing it up. The blood was still spilling out. The second stitch. Yoshie let out a strange sound. She was excited. Even more than during sex. Her eyes were losing focus.

I finished the third stitch, and then the fourth. It took seven stitches in all. I pulled the thread through tight. The gaping wound closed. I knotted the thread.

Blood was all over my fingers, and from my stomach down to my thigh. Yoshie was touching my thigh with her left hand. She made another strange sound, and then she suddenly pushed her face in the blood.

I sat still and waited until Yoshie finished masturbating.

Then I turned on the shower and washed off the blood with cold water. While I was at it, I threw some water on Yoshie's face.

We made a fine pair, I thought. I started thinking that maybe I had let myself get stabbed so that I could show her some real blood.

I applied a towel to the wound.

I went into the living room and sat down on the sofa.

"I'll bring you something for that," she said, taking off her wet clothes. Yoshie had calmed down enough to speak.

She had some antiseptic and gauze in her first aid kit. Once the blood had stopped, I changed the towel for the gauze that I'd soaked in antiseptic.

Yoshie saw the wound and made that strange sound again.

"Once is enough."

"Fine...." Her tone was cool.

"My jacket's okay, but my pants are bloody. Clean them up for me, and press them. I have to wear them tomorrow, too."

"I'll do it right away." Holding my pants, Yoshie disappeared into the bathroom. It was only the area around my belt that was soiled, and I could hide the smaller stains under my jacket. Yoshie didn't come out for a while.

The bleeding was stopping. But now it was starting to hurt. As far as I could tell, he hadn't done any damage to my innards. I knew he didn't have the strength to cut that deep.

I sat up straight. Times like that, I used to beat the guy up within an inch of his life. This time I just kicked the guy once. Maybe I was getting old.

Yoshie came out of the bathroom and took out an iron.

I removed the bloody gauze and taped a clean one to the wound.

"You have an extra shirt?"

"Two. They've both just been cleaned."

I'd taken off my tie and it was in the breast pocket of my jacket.

"I'm going to sleep for a while. If I'm not up by seven, wake me. You got any cotton? If not, a sheet will do. I need to wrap something tight around my waist, like this. Rip it up to about this size." I held up my hands to indicate the width. Then I dove into Yoshie's bed.

I couldn't fall asleep right away because of the pain.

Live like a dog. Die like a dog. Then I suddenly remembered where that came from.

It was from the Boss, the Old Man. The first time I met him, I was nineteen. "You're like a dog. You're a stray dog." The Boss was young back then. He had so much ambition that you felt you could bounce off it.

For some reason, I'd taken to the phrase: like a dog. I wanted to live like a dog, and die like one. I wanted to ever since he said that about me.

I'd fallen asleep before I knew it. I was being shaken. It was seven o'clock.

I shaved, changed the dressing on the wound, and wrapped the torn sheet around me. The stitch was sewn up and I could wrap it tightly around my stomach a number of times.

My jacket and pants were neatly pressed. I was well-dressed. I felt pain shoot through my side, but I was used to it. In other words, he hadn't gotten to my guts.

"You're a strange woman, you know." I'd meant to tell her that she and I were a good match. "I bet you'd get even more excited if I'm stabbed all the way through and squirm around in pain."

"You angry?"

"No."

"I was surprised myself, but I couldn't help it."

"It's fine. I need to be treated like that. I'm just a dog."
There was no way Yoshie'd know what I meant.

I sipped at the coffee she'd poured out for me and took
a bite of toast.

"You don't look so good."

I'd lost blood. I probably looked worse than usual. It
was perfect for what I had to do next.

"So you really sew up your own stitches."

"We *yakuza* lick our own wounds. That's what we're
like." I got up. I tried to put on my shoes and felt pain
shoot through my side again. I noticed a blood stain on my
shoe.

"You coming back here tonight?"

"You don't ask a *yakuza* those kinds of questions," I
said, shoving my foot into the shoe.

I went outside. I couldn't tell where the fight had taken
place last night. The guardrail went a long way.

If I went out on the main street, I could easily hail a
cab. But I continued along the road along the river for a
while before I went out to the main street.

Live like a dog and die like one. Nothing had changed.
I've lived the life of a dog. I wasn't anything else.

I got in a cab.

It was a clear day. The cab weaved through a city that
was growing brighter in the morning sun.

Four young guys were standing in front of the office.

"Who are you?"

There was one I didn't recognize.

"He's Kaneko. He'll start out by helping us with the cleaning. Brother Sugimoto brought him along," one of them explained. The boy bowed deeply.

"He's like a stray dog," I said, and turned my back on him. The office had already been cleaned.

"It's the Clan funeral. Do your best. Don't go around doing anything that will embarrass the Boss," Sugimoto said, coming out from the back. They replied loud and clear and bowed their heads.

"Should we go?" Sugimoto got up and walked out first.

The ink-black Mercedes. The dog was proudly holding the door open.

"Look like that when it's your turn to die, got it?"

"Yes!" he answered eagerly.

I got in the Mercedes and took out a cigarette. Sugimoto held out a light.

The Mercedes started rolling. I slowly blew out a cloud of smoke and closed my eyes. Nothing came to mind.